MW01673456

Above all, for Barbara, who loved me, who believed in me, and said that "I could and I would." I love you and miss you so much. You were everything to me. The best partner ever.
Also for Rev. Dr. John Trevor Wortley, the best professor/ teacher ever.
And, of course, Robert E. Howard.

1176

Stephen S. Bondar

TRANSLATOR'S NOTE:

The following is a preliminary translation into contemporary English of a document recently discovered in a private archive in northern England, and currently on loan to the Bodleian Library, Oxford University.

The document purports to be a letter from one Eadric, an English warrior who had taken service in the famed Varangian Guard in Constantinople during the reign of the Byzantine emperor Manuel I Comnenus (r. 1143 – 80), to a sister who is never actually named. Notwithstanding its late date (internal evidence suggests that if the document is not a fabrication, it must have been penned sometime after 1176, but before or in early 1179), it is written in what can only be termed solid Middle English, reminiscent in places of pre–Norman Conquest epics such as *Beowulf* and *The Battle of Maldon*, even though it is anything but a poem. By the dates in question, one would have expected the letter to have been composed in either Latin or Norman French, but the author clearly self-identifies as an Anglo-Saxon, and the implication is that his sister does as well, despite being married (unhappily and probably against her wishes) to a Norman nobleman. Her situation would not have been unique; after the initial ravages of the Conquest (1066), many of the old Anglo-Saxon families had been able to preserve some of their wealth and position through intermarriage with the new Norman aristocracy, the reigning monarch Henry II Plantagenet (r. 1154 – 89) by this time even having Saxon blood in him. The sister's marriage seems to have been just such a one, arranged by an older brother for whom she, and certainly Eadric, held little but disdain. One is tempted to speculate that Eadric may even have written the letter in Middle English as a kind of code, rendering it incomprehensible to the majority even of the other literate members of his sister's household. Although much of the information in the letter is intended to be passed on, it also contains some comments of a candid and personal nature that, were they to come to the attention of the wrong persons, while they would have been unlikely to have put the sister in actual physical danger, would certainly have rendered her already uncomfortable domestic situation even worse. Again, however, this is speculation.

We know nothing more of Eadric beyond that which he himself tells us, or we can legitimately infer from the letter, as there does not seem to be any other identifiable mention of him in any other known source. As to the letter's provenance, all that is presently known is that its current owner cites a family tradition of its having been found in a hidden (secret?) niche between the wall and floor of what had likely been a bedchamber in an ancient manor–house in the vicinity of York, together with a handful of silver coins and a silver ring or bracelet, in the 1870's. The property had been abandoned for decades when her great-great- great-grandfather had purchased it, and had fallen into considerable disrepair, hence her ancestor's decision to undertake extensive renovations, during the course of which the discovery took place. The fate of the coins and jewelry is unknown; this is unfortunate, as the coins (by their dates of issue) would have been helpful in at least determining an absolute earliest date on which we could say for certain that someone might have seen and been aware of the document's existence, although of course it may have been placed/hidden in the niche even before the coins were deposited therein. Naturally, should any of the coins have dated from substantially after the late twelfth century, that would beg the question as to why the letter continued to be kept hidden (which it almost certainly was, considering the location of its discovery) well after anyone who could have suffered prejudice due to its contents had long since paid the debt of all flesh. Alas, this mystery may never be solved.

That the letter is genuine, I have little doubt. While it has yet to undergo a proper forensic analysis regarding, e.g., its ink and the parchment sheets themselves, to the eyes of both myself and other mediaevalists who have studied dozens, if not hundreds of centuries-old documents, it appears on initial observation to fit the bill. This, of course, is not to deny that there have been numerous instances of documents that distinguished scholars had thought genuine having subsequently been proven to have been clever forgeries. However, I submit that I have additional support for my position, beyond that already mentioned.

First, the language the letter is written in. If it were a forgery (like the so-called "Prester John letter" that it actually mentions in its text, and that most scholars agree was penned primarily for entertainment purposes), then why would it not have been written in Latin or Norman French, which by the late twelfth century would have made it accessible to a much wider audience? The text purports to inform us that it was the very sister whom Eadric is writing to who had taught him to read and write in their ancestral tongue.

Second, there is the very script itself. The penmanship is by far the worst I have ever seen in such a document. This leads me to believe that not only is the document genuine, but that Eadric actually wrote it in his own hand, rather than engaging a scribe and dictating it, as was common practice among educated laymen throughout the Middle Ages. And that educated Eadric was, at least more than most, we can discern from his vocabulary alone. Yet the handwriting is crabbed and uneven; the work of a person who rarely had occasion to put quill to parchment, if at all. It is certainly not the hand of one who wrote for a living. While Eadric appears to have been very comfortable with words, he was not accustomed to writing them down. Again, as with the language itself, my best guess is that Eadric refrained from hiring a scribe on account of the personal and sensitive nature of some of the communiqué's contents.

Third, there does not appear to be anything fanciful or deliberately fabricated in the letter's account of events — ones Eadric states that he was not only an eyewitness to, but participated in. The better part of the letter is a detailed description of the battle of Myriocephalon [17-18 September 1176], and it squares well with our established sources regarding that disastrous event, namely the work of the Byzantine historian Nicetas Choniates[1], and a letter from Emperor Manuel himself that a Byzantine ambassador presented to King Henry II.[2] Indeed, Eadric goes into considerable (and gruesome) detail; saying that his sister has "a warrior's heart", he spares none of the horrors that he witnessed on those days.

Why did Eadric feel such a pressing need to inform his sister so graphically of the battle's grisly particulars and its aftermath?

Clearly, Eadric and his sister are of noble Anglo-Saxon descent, and as such are the scions of a warrior aristocracy. While no specific titles or ancestors are mentioned, Eadric's sister was married to a baron. He himself was a younger son in a regime of strict primogeniture, where many such chose to seek their fortunes in Outremer (the "lands beyond the sea", as the Crusader States of the Middle East were known) or otherwise as mercenaries. Others turned to the Church or the law; such may have been parental intentions for Eadric at first, as we have already noted his apparently above-average level of education, although we cannot safely base too much upon that, as it is well-known that literacy was quite common among both sexes of the Anglo-Saxon upper classes. Perhaps Eadric's path changed when it became obvious that his temperament was better suited to the battlefield than the pulpit or the courts. Again, however, this is only speculation.

What *is* certain is that Eadric held the martial ideals of his class very dearly, not only with regard to his own conduct and abilities, but those of others as well. Because of this — and I will not belabour the point, as Eadric's words speak clearly enough for themselves — he felt a need to offer a corrective to the widely-held

Western European view of the Byzantines that can be summed up in the oft-referenced phrase "perfidious Greeks", an unfortunate characterization which has coloured historical opinions both lay and professional right down to the present time, and even given the very term "byzantine" (when used as an adjective) a decidedly negative connotation. He even states an intention to someday commission a translation of a general history of the Byzantine Empire, though whether he ever did, or if so, what became of it, we have no knowledge.

Simply put, for the westerner, be he Frankish, German, Norman, or any other, the overwhelmingly typical stereotype of the Byzantine was that of an effeminate pleasure-seeker who could not be trusted, and who preferred to pay others to fight his battles rather than to do so himself, as a result of the cowardice that was a natural product of his moral, as well as in many cases physical, inferiority. He was, after all, too busy taking baths and adorning himself with fine raiments and trinkets (as well as perfumes and scented oils) "in the manner of a woman", when he wasn't debating or expounding obscure and incomprehensible points of theology — or planning how best to stab you in the back at the first reasonable opportunity. The fact that the eastern (Orthodox) and western (Roman Catholic) churches had been in a state of schism since 1054 did not help.

Eadric, however, knew the Byzantines for what they truly were, and had nothing but respect for their martial prowess, although he was well aware of their reputation (and we must admit it) capacity for intrigue. He had taken service with the storied Varangian Guard, an elite unit recruited strictly from foreigners who were extremely unlikely to become involved in any sort of political plotting or attempts at palace coups, as they had no local interests beyond the Emperor's well-being — they answered solely to a special Byzantine officer called the *hetaireiarch,* whose only responsibility they were, and through him, to the Emperor — and were also paid extremely well. The Varangians, who only ever numbered a few thousand, were thus entrusted with guarding the Emperor, his family, and the Imperial precincts within Constantinople, as well as accompanying the Emperor on campaign. Although when the unit was first formed under the Emperor Basil II (r. 976-1025), nicknamed the "Bulgar-slayer", it was composed almost exclusively of Norsemen and Russians, it had, by Eadric's time, a significant Anglo-Saxon element to it (possibly even a majority), as post-1066, many young warriors in Eadric's position found themselves having to seek fame and fortune far from their ancestral homeland. How long Eadric had served we do not know, only that he had, and had then undertaken the long (and often arduous) journey home, only to find his domestic situation in England so intolerable that he decided to return to service in Constantinople. We do know that at some point he had been offered command of fifty men, which would probably have made him the equivalent of a commissioned officer today; he had, however, refused the position, choosing instead to remain one of the most trusted of all, those who served in the Emperor's immediate presence. It is to our good fortune that he chose thus, because he would not otherwise have been able to give us the account that he has.

It would be difficult indeed to overestimate the significance of Myriocephalon for the Christian east (writ large to include the Byzantine Empire as well as the Crusader States), especially when viewed in conjunction with the Knights Templars' disastrous defeat by Saladin at the Horns of Hattin the following year. Yet there is now considerable debate among scholars as to whether the Empire's misfortunes over the next three decades were an *inevitable* result of Myriocephalon, or if the damage it sustained was in fact less crippling than has traditionally been believed. After all, Byzantine forces returned to the field the following year, recording several successes (albeit on a much smaller scale than Myriocephalon, which has been said to have been the single biggest military undertaking by a Christian monarch in the twelfth century) including decisive victories in the Maeander river valley and at Panasium, the latter under Manuel's personal command,

and at which Eadric was again a witness and participant. Also in 1177, Manuel sent a fleet of seventy warships to Acre, intended as naval support for a joint expedition with the Kingdom of Jerusalem against Egypt. While it failed to materialize (through no fault of Manuel's) this was clearly a projection of power by an empire that was far from being on its knees.

For whatever it is worth, I gravitate towards the view of those scholars who believe that regardless of any later successes, Manuel returned from Myriocephalon essentially a broken man, and I respectfully submit that Eadric's observations support this position. Manuel's physical health deteriorated rapidly between Myriocephalon and his premature death of a sudden illness in 1180. Despite this, he spent a significant part of that time in relentless campaigning, which probably only helped to wear him down. While of course we have no direct or specific assessment of Manuel's mental health over those final four years, the overwhelming consensus is that he was never quite the same after the battle; perhaps especially not after that terrible moment of doubt and near-panic in the dark hours of the night of September 17, which Eadric describes so graphically.

In any event, few would dispute that Manuel's early death was a calamity for the Empire. He left his throne to a child (Alexius II, described by Choniates as having been "of a singularly vicious disposition"[3]), whose titular reign lasted only until 1183, shortly after which he was strangled at the behest of his much older cousin, the infamous Andronicus I, who was in turn torn to pieces by the mob in 1185, in the course of *his* deposition in the coup that brought Isaac II Angelus out of prison and onto the throne.

That the Empire's fortunes only proceeded from bad to worse under the six emperors who reigned between 1180 and the debacle of 1204, which it survived only as a shadow of a shadow of what it had been under the emperors of the Amorian/Macedonian dynasty, is beyond dispute. As I have already stated above, I am of the respectful opinion that this situation was largely a result of Manuel's early passing without leaving a competent (or even principled) successor. If indeed his decline can be viewed as part (in addition to the staggering, although as stated above, probably not completely crippling, losses of blood and treasure) of the fallout of Myriocephalon, it becomes all the more vital for us to understand what it was that Manuel witnessed and experienced on those days, especially if it may in one way or another have hounded him into an early grave.

Here, however, I feel compelled to admit that, even in possession of a firsthand account such as the one presented here, it is very likely that those of us who have never been on the field of battle (in *any* epoch) will fall far short of a true fullness of appreciation or indeed, comprehension. John Haldon has pointed out in his monograph on the Byzantine military[4] that regardless of century or level of technology, probably the most severely traumatic experience a human being can undergo is combat. Post-traumatic stress disorder resultant therefrom may have only finally have been fully recognized (and named) in the twentieth century, but it is doubtless older than recorded history, and has been with us since men first faced each other with crude stone clubs.

That Manuel experienced combat on numerous occasions is beyond question. Regardless of his well-known penchant for luxury, it seems clear (at least in my respectful view), that in his heart of hearts, he was a soldier-emperor in the mold of his father and grandfather before him. While it was impossible for him to have been in all places at all times, he preferred commanding his armies in person to remaining in the (relative) safety of Constantinople, and he did not command from the rear. He was beloved by his men, and generally respected by allies and enemies alike. While denigrated (as was almost *de rigueur* for Byzantine emperors) by the Latins of Western Europe, he was held in considerable (if possibly grudging) regard by those of Outremer.

The present introduction has gone on long enough, especially considering this to be a preliminary translation. I offer it in the pages of this journal (both print and electronic) in the hopeful (if also somewhat anxious) anticipation of criticism and commentary from colleagues around the world, as such will be invaluable to me in the completion of a definitive edition, which I expect to present in approximately a twelvemonth. Such will be accompanied by a much more detailed introduction and (probably fairly extensive) notes.[5]

A note on transliteration: for present purposes, I have chosen to render even technical Greek terms (in the places Eadric uses them) into their closest modern English equivalents, or at least into the loan-words most commonly employed in English [*eg. trebuchet* = (a type of) catapult], and therefore likely to be familiar to most students of mediaeval history. The forthcoming edition will contain footnotes in all such instances, including explanation as well as potential alternative translations and any possible significance of such. Similarly, I have rendered proper names in their traditional, rather than strictly phonetic transliterations (*eg.* Comnenus, not Komnenos; Nureddin, not Nūr-ad-Dīn).

I have also taken the liberty of editing for appropriate modern English punctuation, particularly the use of parentheses and quotation marks. Again, all such instances will be noted in the comprehensive edition. Finally, I have split Eadric's narrative into paragraphs that are in my opinion consistent with modern usage. The blame for any unclarities or ambiguities arising from these editorial decisions should be laid at my feet, not those of the original author.

And now, without further *adieu*, other than the deepest thanks to Oxford University, the Bodleian Library and the staff thereof, I will stand aside, and give the floor to Eadric.

To my beloved sister, greetings. I pray with all my heart that this letter finds you well and whole, and as happy as can be, considering the situation our dear elder bootlicking brother —a murrain[6] seize him —has put you into. May our Lord hold you and your little Henry safe in His hands. I could not wish for a finer nephew. Even at six winters, it is clear to anyone who has eyes to see with, that your good Saxon blood prevails in him over that of your husband the baron, that pig of a Norman whom our own brother married you to despite all of your tears and my entreaties. I beg that you forgive me for not doing more, but fraternal ties of blood —and little else — prevented me from doing what I would have preferred to a man who would rather preserve his fortune by selling his sister's hand to a dog than by selling his sword in Outremer, or just taking the Cross[7] like so many better men before him. I will not play Cain to his Pharaoh.[8] God will judge him — and me — accordingly. Yet sturdy young Henry is a bright spot and a gift, and I pray that one day I too will be blessed with a son or daughter half as fine as him, although when, where, and with whom, I do not know. Perhaps mine will be half Greek?

Should you think to yourself that I write the last line only partly in jest, then, as usual, you perceive correctly. As you already know, I have decided to return to service with the Varangians in Constantinople. By the time this letter is in your hands, I should be already at sea, on my way back to the one *true* empire of the Romans, as they justifiably call it.[9] I may well even remain there to live out my remaining days after my soldiering ones are over, if I can obtain permission to settle, and if the situation there does not deteriorate (as I fear it might). Certainly, as you already know, there is no place for me in England, though it be the land of my birth.

Please, I beg you, do not be over-vexed with our dear old Agnes for keeping this letter from you until now. She was a second mother to us both, and the best lady's maid ever to both our own mother and now yourself, I'm sure you will agree. I knew I could trust her when I insisted upon her oath — against her own wishes, and I am sure you can imagine the fuss she raised — to keep it concealed until a fortnight after my departure. You had already, dear sister, presented me with all of your arguments intended to persuade me to stay, and I had, with a heavier heart than you know, rejected them all. We have said our farewells, and I did not wish to give you another opportunity, as I feared that, at the last moment, my love for both you and Henry might have swayed me, if not to remain for good, then at least to delay my leaving. That would have been unlikely to have turned out well for any of us.

I hope that I did not inconvenience you overmuch by taking so long to depart after our final embrace. You had said that you could not bear further and more prolonged goodbyes, and that you would remain in your quarters until the gatehouse had seen the back of me, and you stayed true to your word. I am afraid I deceived you somewhat — and for that I beseech your indulgence — when I told you that I had some affairs to settle before I could go, and that they would take three or four days. The only affairs I needed to settle were to prepare these words, and bind Agnes to my confidence.

I leave this because I feel that I owe it not only to you, but to my battle-brothers across the sea, *most especially* those Greek ones that the brainless louts who wear your husband's arms constantly malign, without ever having met one in person. Because of the remarks I have already made, and others I still intend to make, it would of course be best for your own situation (at the very least in terms of whatever domestic harmony you can hope to have with that braying ass) if your eyes were the only ones to see this letter. I strongly suggest that you either hide, or better yet, destroy it after reading it. Agnes, God bless her, will take this —and probably many other —secrets to her grave, as you well know. She has more honour than all of those so-called noblemen in your husband's — and our dear brother's — circles together, and it is surely a warrior's heart that beats in her breast, as in yours.

And it is because I know that you are possessed of such a heart, and have been since we were children at our games, when you always wanted to join us boys in our stick-fights and leave your poppets to the other girls, that I am about to relate things to you that I would never think of describing to any other female, saving perhaps only Agnes. For these are not merely matters not generally raised in the company of ladies, but are the stuff that stalks through the nightmares of hard men. And yet I trust that you will find some way to relate them in at least a general manner to counter the drivel and outright lies that are bruited about in England, and indeed throughout most of western Christendom — for I found little difference in the other lands that I travelled through — regarding the Roman Empire and its "little Greeks", as that ridiculous "letter" from the so-called Prester John calls them.

For me, it beggars belief that a make-believe missive from a make-believe monarch of the far, far east, in whose kingdom rivers flow with precious stones, there are worms that dwell in fire and fish that abound in dry deserts, and in whose palace this king "who reigns supreme and exceeds in riches, virtue, and power all creatures who dwell under Heaven" daily feeds thirty thousand men at a dining table carved from a single emerald, and endless other nonsense could be as widely read, recited, quoted from, and discussed as I have found it to be in dining-halls and around campfires across the entire west of Christendom. I have encountered not a few who actually believe in the existence of this "Prester" or "Priest" John and his kingdom (where also poverty does not exist, and — ironically — anyone who tells a lie is instantly struck dead) in spite of this letter's obviously being a fable and a forgery. While there are known (by the Greeks) to actually be Christians far to the farthest east, in the place called India, or Cathay perhaps, and there are even credible rumours of Christian chieftains and possibly even a king somewhere, no grown man in his right mind could possibly believe that there is one in whose palace archbishops, other kings, and patriarchs serve as butlers, as this letter would have it. And also, by the by, although these easterners may be Christians by their own declaration, they are in fact likely to be followers of the teachings of the heretic Nestorius, condemned centuries ago. The letter itself — no doubt deliberately — is insultingly addressed to the emperor Manuel by name, referring to him as the "governor" of the "little Greeks" as though *he* were no more than someone's steward or chamberlain.

Speaking of chamberlains, I should interject here that your

dear husband's should count himself fortunate that he is still possessed of any teeth after he expressed his — completely uninformed, yet typical — opinion to me two days back of the Greeks with whom I have stood back-to-back on the field of slaughter, and to more than one of whom I owe my life. I have learned amongst those very Greeks that killing someone over a passing (and sometimes merely perceived) insult is not only not Christian behaviour, but not even the behaviour of an adult of balanced mind. Yet I was sorely tempted to give that windbag the pommel of my sword, if not the actual blade. However, I restrained myself once more, as I have almost daily — sometimes more than once — since I have been here.

But my patience wears thin, and I fear for your sake, as I have already said, that my forbearance is dangerously close to its limit. Your husband's retainers expect me to laugh with them at those whom I have fought alongside, marched with, half-starved with, bled with — and out of concern for you and Henry I have endured their prattle with clenched teeth behind the thin smiles I have forced myself to muster, all the while keeping my hand hidden in the folds of my cloak or behind my back so no one could see my fingers curling into a fist.

They boast endlessly of how their fellow Norman Roger, the King of Sicily surpasses Manuel in all matters of nobility, martial prowess, and manliness itself, and of how easily he will conquer the Romans in the war they all expect (and hope) this Roger will start. Myself , I know little of this man, and therefore will not stoop to casting aspersions on his character, but my advice to him would be to inquire of Kilidj Arslan, the Sultan of Iconium (the victor at Myriocephalon) as to just how *easy* it is to best the Romans on the field of battle. I tell you, on our mother's grave, he would not like the answer. And now also, made bold by the Empire's misfortune, that German dog Barbarossa sends letters and envoys to Constantinople demanding that Manuel recognize *him* as Emperor of the Romans and swear fealty to him as a vassal!

Of course, Manuel will never recognize this ridiculous

claim, which does nothing but highlight the German king's ignorance of history. Regardless of any of his ancestors' claims, the capital of the Roman Empire was moved many centuries ago from Old Rome by Saint Constantine, the first Christian emperor, to the city founded by and named by him, Constantinople, the New Rome. There is no other Roman Empire or Emperor, regardless of what (and may God forgive me if I sin in saying this) the Pope says.

I know these facts because I spent a good part of my free time in Constantinople learning about the history of the empire I was serving. I suppose this came from the curiosity and love of learning that our mother, who taught you the letters that, bless your sweet soul, you in turn taught me, instilled in both of us. Thanks to her, I cannot imagine living in a place without wishing to know at least a little something about how it came to be the way that it is, or how and even why it might be different from other places. And thanks to you, I can read not only Latin, but our own good ancestors' Saxon, in which I write these words, though I fear, alas, that it is dying out.

Nevertheless, being unlettered in Greek, I was unable to read any of the many histories of the Roman Empire which have been written in that language. Hence, as I told you, I hired a scribe to read a couple of them to me, and help me with words or phrases that were beyond the spoken Greek that I have. (These were many more than you might expect because, as the scribe informed me, it was the style for most of the learned authors to write in a somewhat archaic form of the language, in order, it seems, to appear even *more* learned. In this I *will* concede pretentiousness on the part of certain Greeks, particularly a man called Psellus.) It was actually quite hard work, but more than worthwhile for me for the knowledge I gained, and certainly worthwhile for the scribe, considering the coin I put out. (That was not a complaint, dear sister; as mother always told us, no price can be placed upon knowledge.) Also, the scribe was a good and kind man, not conceited in any way, and supporting a wife and six children. He was the same man I told you about that I had hired to read the Greek books on military science to me, and to make me the private translation of my favourite one (which I showed to you), believed to have originally been written two hundred years ago by the emperor Nicephorus Phocas[10], one of the Empire's greatest generals. (And yet the majority of your husband's men find it surprising that literacy is virtually a prerequisite for promotion to even the middling ranks of the Roman regular army.) This scribe, by name Theodoulos, told me repeatedly of his gratitude for the commission, as it would keep his family for almost half a year, should he for some reason lose his regular employment as tutor to the children of a wealthy, but ill-tempered spice merchant. Mother would have been grateful too, for as a result of the time and money I put into this, I spent somewhat less of both in the taverns than I otherwise might have, like many of my comrades!

In fact, I would like someday to commission a full translation (into Latin, so that it would be comprehensible throughout the western lands as well as Outremer — if there still is an Outremer by then, Christ forgive me for saying that, but recent Saracen[11] successes have been alarming) of one of the most complete histories. This would be dear, but I should be well able to afford it by the time I retire from service, especially if that promotion I told you about is still available to me. I am already paid very well, and it would increase considerably. I would have been in command of fifty men, but I declined the position when it was offered to me — a little more than two years ago — because I wanted to remain in the place I had already earned in the Emperor's immediate presence in the line of battle as one of his personal bodyguards. Nevertheless, I am older now, and should start thinking more about my later years — of course, never a certainty, especially not for a soldier — and maybe a family (especially if I can find myself some dark little beauty — but she'd have to have a heart to match her looks, and some wits in her head as well). I will speak to the current *hetaireiarch* upon my return.

That would all be my choice, should our Lord will and permit it, for I cannot stay in England. If I tried to, I would eventually either kill or maim one or more of these half-wits regardless of the restraint I have learned abroad, or get physically sick unto my own death from holding in my anger. But as I said, the situation in Constantinople when I left was becoming uncertain.

Yes, mistakes were made, and a major battle was lost, but the Emperor avenged it quickly, and did not bow to the Sultan's demands to dismantle all of the fortifications we had just rebuilt on the frontier, most especially not the most important ones, at a place called Dorylaeum. Within less than a twelvemonth of the events I am about to relate, I was again at the *Basileus*' (the Greek word for emperor) side when we captured Panasium from the infidel, our arms and our hearts braced by tidings of our comrades' victory to the east — a force under the noble Grand Domestic (the highest military rank after the Emperor himself) John Vatatzes had trapped and almost completely destroyed a Seljuk army as it tried to make a forced crossing back over the Maeander River while laden with booty from raiding. Nor did the navy lay idle — at least not by its own or the Emperor's choice. Around the same time as these successful land engagements, some seventy warships were sent to Acre to be staged from there in an attack on Damietta that never took place, through no fault on our (Imperial) side of the bargain. The land force which was to be provided by the Crusaders never was, I heard mostly because of the Count of Flanders, and so our Roman galleys wasted an entire season in harbour.[12]

The frontiers are not what make me worry, at least not any more than usual, but rather the situation in Constantinople, especially in the palace. The Emperor has never seemed the same since that terrible day and night in those passes, not on the days that followed on the march home that we had we had to make past the mutilated and desecrated bodies of our fallen comrades, nor really ever since. Even publicly, he seems different, though I am sure he is trying very hard not to. But because of my position — I have stood guard at the doors of the Imperial bedchamber, the Imperial family's private dining rooms, and others of the palace's most intimate precincts — I can say with certainty that the Emperor is *not* the man he was before. His appetite (previously that of a dedicated gourmand) is poor, and he does not sleep well, and constantly appears tired, and lost in or distracted by his own thoughts, even during discussions of affairs of state and audiences given to foreign ambassadors. Whereas he often used to participate wholeheartedly in festivities and games like polo, even to the point where some Greeks criticized his behaviour as unbecoming the Imperial dignity, he now seems to take little joy in these things, when he even bothers with them at all. He used to be filled with self-assurance (which many mistook for vanity or arrogance); now he endlessly questions his own judgement, and hesitates and turns himself inside out over the smallest of decisions. He drinks more wine than he used to, or is healthy. Anyone can see that his health — and I believe his spirit — is failing. It pains me to witness this, as I know the man he was before, and I love him as I would a blood relative, and so did most of my comrades. Perhaps as the sort of elder brother I would have wished for the both of us to have had.

The Emperor was, in a way, not one, but two fine men. At home, he was a diligent ruler, deeply concerned with the prosperity of his empire; he did not just sit on his throne while his appointed ministers looked after matters of state for him, but took a personal interest in all these things, including the law courts and the affairs of the Church. And no foreigner who visited his court could have left it with any doubt that he had been at the wealthiest and most glorious such in the world (unless the idiot actually believed in Prester John). The Emperor's joy at hosting embassies and putting on spectacular entertainments, including tournaments after our western manner (which no previous Roman emperor had done, and some Greeks actually found distasteful) was unfeigned. Manuel enjoyed state ceremonies, appearances before the crowd in the Hippodrome, sponsoring poets, rhetors, musicians, and artists, and setting the tone for his court in all manner of things. He *enjoyed* being the ruler of an empire over a thousand years old, whose capital is known amongst the nations as the Queen of Cities, where, for enough money, anything can be had, from any corner of the world.

You may think, sister, that this is not entirely the kind of ruler we Saxons were raised to respect, and you would be right, if that was all that there was to Manuel Comnenus. In fact, there are quite a few, both westerners (particularly Normans) and Greeks as well, who think exactly that. They dismiss him as a lover of luxury, a libertine, a dandy, essentially an overgrown child and a wastrel. Myself, I do not think this really fair, not only because of all that I am about to relate, but also because I have come to believe that embodying the glory, majesty, and wealth of the Empire is one of the duties of the *basileus*. Although there are few who would seriously argue against that, there are too many who are convinced that that is *all* this emperor is, and that his chief concerns are an unending parade of pageants, exotic dishes, fine wines, and beautiful women — and let us not forget garments dripping with gold, diamonds, rubies, sapphires, and the like.

But the soldiers know different. They know the other Emperor Manuel Comnenus, battle-hardened and cut from the same bloodstained cloth as his father and grandfather before him. Who marches out to the frontiers of the Empire with his men over and over again, year in, year out. Who commands his guard personally as one of the most important and effective units in his army, and does not lead from the rear nor observe the battle from a distant position of safety while his men shed their blood for him. He bleeds with them, and shares their privations on campaign. He leads foraging parties in hostile territory. If the least of his men goes on half-rations, so does he. When haste has been essential, he has abandoned even the purple Imperial tent and its trappings when we made up extra miles on forced marches by torchlight or a full moon. More than once has he slept on a bed of hay chaff with only his own upturned shield for a pillow. When in a marching camp, he has taken turns leading patrols around the perimeter, stopping at random to speak with ordinary soldiers and inquire as to their welfare and that of their families. I know this, because I walked some of those patrols with him myself. These things I tell you now, let no one say I am spinning some saga or panegyric for entertainment in firelit halls on cold winter nights, I saw them with my own eyes. Not only saw, but lived them. When we refortified Dorylaeum, he took part in the manual labour, moving the first stones with his own hands. Those of us who carry arms in his name know that beneath whatever shining raiments he dons in the palace, his body bears not a feather's-weight of blubber, but rather the scars of a veteran soldier, some earned before he was even of an age to grow a proper beard.

And it always seems, at least to me, that the transformation between the one Emperor Manuel and the other took place in little more than a few heartbeats, as we passed through the gate, entering or leaving the City, almost as though by some kind of benign magic. One man entered on this side of the towering land walls, the second passed out the other, just like that. From the resplendence of the purple-born prince[13] who reigns from a golden throne to the grit of the warrior who has bested Serbian chieftains in single combat, and is said to have (before my time) once captured a Turk by dragging him from the saddle by his hair.

There are ceremonies, prayers, and blessings associated with an emperor's entries and exits into and out of the City, as well as most of his other public activities, many of which have been laid down in writing in some book generations ago.[14] But I have been able to see that this particular Emperor has his own additional custom that I believe helps him make this quick transition between two very different manners of life. As we pass beneath the stone, he takes a number of long, deep breaths, and casts his eyes downward for a moment, speaking what must be a short prayer so quietly that I cannot identify it, even from less than ten paces away. Then he raises his eyes again just as we come out one side or the other.

But something has changed with him, and not for the better. In the City, his old gaiety is gone, replaced by constant, and often distracted brooding. I also know he now prefers to be in the field, although he used to enjoy both manners of life equally. He campaigns even more tirelessly than before, sometimes even subjecting himself to additional privations, beyond those required by actual circumstances. I make no claim to being a wise man, but I think anyone would be convinced that he is somehow punishing himself for something that he cannot forgive himself for, regardless of whether God or any other mortal might. I fear that he may be slowly killing himself with the grueling pace that he is subjecting himself to. Even worse, I wonder if that might not be his intention, whether he knows it or not.

If he should die, or I return to Constantinople to find that he has died already, I know not what I shall do then. No way could I remain there, as I cannot see myself serving (at least not with a clear conscience and without a heavy heart) any of those who are likely to succeed him.

The only direct heir of his body is his son Alexius, who is a child, which would of course result in a regency. (And mark you, even if he were of mature years, this Alexius would likely make a terrible ruler, as he is already known by all to be a cruel and unpleasant boy, displaying few if any of the traits of the grandfather who bore the same name. The sort of boy who pulls the wings off of flies and the legs off of spiders — a lot like your husband, I am sorry to say.) The Empress Maria, Alexius' mother, may try to rule as regent for her son by herself, but most seem to doubt it, although I am told that that women have done so several times in the past. And this would be a good thing were she a woman of your character, or our mother's. But she is not, and anyway, almost everyone believes that she will seek support from whomever is her paramour of the moment.

I should explain to you that she [Maria] is much younger than Manuel, his second wife after the death of German-born Bertha of blessed memory. Not only did Manuel need to marry again in order to produce an heir — he had none from Bertha — but apparently he was "intoxicated" by the beauty of this Crusader princess, Maria of Antioch, whose charms were celebrated throughout Outremer, and marriage with whom was also a very good political alliance. But she is young, and beautiful (as are many poisonous snakes), and also very willful. Her affairs after her son's birth are an open secret, and in his current state, the Emperor seems either to take no notice, or just not to care. She is also smart, in a selfish sort of way, and knows that being an outsider (a Latin), she will need support from some powerful Greek faction if she wants to rule for very long. When I left, her favour was given to another Alexius, a close relative of the Emperor's, who is not loved by the populace, which will only encourage his rivals, of whom there are several within the Imperial family, not to mention other ambitious men outside it. The most dangerous of all of them (because he *would* — I know not how or why, because he is a two-faced scoundrel — have wide support from the ordinary citizens) is an old weasel of an Imperial cousin, Andronicus Comnenus, who has plotted against Manuel more than once already. (No mere rumour — he has actually been *convicted* of treason, but Manuel, out of sympathy for the ties of blood and their common ancestry, pardoned this dog instead of permanently exiling, or better yet, executing him.)

And whoever takes control of the palace, young Alexius will only be in their way. Even if it is Maria, I do not for a moment believe that any natural maternal love will outweigh her other lusts, particularly that for power, nor the wishes of any of her potential consorts. Although I — strongly — dislike the boy, the heir of Manuel Comnenus' loins deserves better than the garrote that is his likely fate regardless of which adult ends up on top of this wretched pile.

I could serve none of them, not after having marched with Manuel. Worse, civil war would be very possible. I could not take a side in such a thing, even in the name of the legitimate heir (particularly because, as I have said, he is a detestable young fellow by nature, and would anyway only be a figurehead for another's ambitions, likely to be disposed of as soon as it seems safe). I will not shed the blood of men who have stood beside me in the line, nor do I wish to die by the blade or bow of one who by all that is right and decent and honourable I should call friend, be he Greek, Saxon, Norseman, Magyar, Cuman, or anything else.

Should such misfortunes come to pass, I suppose I will travel north across the Black Sea, and up the Dnieper river to take service with one of the princes of Rus, or maybe Galicia. I have served with men from there, and believe that I might be more comfortable among them than even in Palestine, though Palestine is not out of the question. It might well come down to where I can get a ship to sooner!

Whatever happens, sister, I will send you word by some comrade whom I trust, when such a man is travelling your way. Currently, if God has spared a good man and fine soldier, that would be Bjarni Thorsteinson, a good friend whose intended term of service in the Guard should end a few months after my likely date of return. He is a Dane, but with good Saxon blood on his maternal grandmother's side. He will be travelling home to Iceland, and I know he would be happy to go by way of England if I asked him, and promised him the hospitality I know you will graciously provide. I will send a letter with him, or whomever else I might trust to convey my news to you. (I do hope and pray that it can be him.) I also still hope that someday, somehow, I might see you again, face to face, but you know that no matter where I go, you and Henry will be foremost in my heart and in my prayers.

But enough of this. Times flees like a bandit, and I must relate to you the truth of the events that took place two Septembers ago, that you may not be misled by the rubbish that comes out of so many of the ignorant mouths around you. You may yet even be able to correct some of it by passing on the true facts as now related by your brother, who was actually there, and as God is my witness, would not have survived were it not for the "governor of the little Greeks".

To begin with, I must assure you that, regardless of its

critics, this project of the Emperor's was no dream-castle in the sky built of vanity, but was well-grounded in solid strategic thinking. But yes, mistakes — and bad ones — were made, and they cost us dearly. But this campaign itself was a sound idea, possibly unlike some of the Emperor's earlier adventures in Italy. In fact, quite a few of his detractors maintain that had he not squandered men and money on those, he would have had more resources for this campaign, and it might have been successful. While I agree that Asia is far more important than Italy to the Roman Empire of today, I think — no, I am *convinced* — that we had more than enough of everything for this expedition. Our failure lay in tactics, not strategy. (See how many of your husband's men know the difference between those two words.) And I repeat, disaster though it was, it was not one from which the Empire could not, nor cannot yet recover from, with God's grace and good leadership.

The Saracens and Turks are no more united than are the kingdoms and principalities of Europe or Outremer, and frequently fight against one another even more ferociously than they do the Crusaders. They often make peace with Christian powers in order to be able to concentrate on their feuds with fellow Muslims, and even temporary alliances between Muslims and Christians against other Muslims (and sometimes the reverse) are hardly unknown. These are, I admit, more common with the Greeks, which is a big reason why many Crusaders mistrust them.

The situation in the East is far more complicated than most people (even the better-informed ones) in far-away England realize. The continued security of the Roman Empire is threatened not only by the sons of Ishmael, but also by various enemies to the north, as well as our own dear Normans from the west. Sometimes the Emperor has to balance one enemy against another, or even appease one in order to fight another.

The Emperor had thus mostly been at peace with Kilidj [II] Arslan, the Sultan of Iconium, or Rum, as the Hagarenes often insultingly call it (for *Rome*, as though they had conquered the

Roman Empire itself, rather than just part of its territory). Some fifteen or more years back (well before my time), Emperor Manuel had prosecuted some successful campaigns in Anatolia [Asia Minor] against the Sultan, who had then sued for peace on terms favourable to the Empire. In fact, the Sultan was invited to and entertained as a guest in Constantinople while the treaty was drawn up. Not only did this secure (for the time being) Manuel's southern borders in Anatolia, but the Sultan was also required to lend him a contingent of light troops to fight in his Hungarian wars. This peace helped not only Manuel, but also Kilidj, as he was able to rebuild his strength to deal with *his* other enemies, the (also Muslim) Danishmendid princes to his north and east, and the powerful Sultan of Egypt, Nureddin. This peace was also of great benefit to Christians from the West, because one of Kilidj's concessions to Manuel was to allow pilgrims free passage through his territory, hence allowing them to travel in relative safety overland from Constantinople to Palestine and the Holy Land.

But while Manuel concentrated on campaigns in Hungary, Kilidj made the best of his opportunities in Asia, at the expense of the Danishmends, who in their turn appealed to Nureddin as an ally and protector. Ever looking to cast an even longer shadow, Nureddin attacked Arslan's territory in Anatolia, and forced Arslan to negotiate a treaty that made him break his earlier peace with Manuel, because Nureddin made Iconium's fighting the Greeks one of its terms. Knowing of this, and anticipating trouble, Manuel took the initiative by advancing a large force towards the ancient city of Philadelphia in western Anatolia, within days of the border, in which I marched, although there was very little fighting there (I personally saw none). Seeing that Manuel was not taking these threats lightly, Arslan *again* reversed his position, and renewed his treaty with the Roman Empire, breaking the one he had just made with Nureddin.

Nureddin, of course, immediately prepared to attack. But, fortunately as it turned out for Kilidj Arslan, he, Nureddin, died within the year, and his place was taken by his nephew Saladin.

While I am sure that time will show Saladin to be even more of a threat than his uncle (especially to Outremer), Iconium was, at least for a time, spared further danger, because he wanted to strengthen his control of Syria before campaigning any farther from his base of power in Egypt. (And that is why he *will* be dangerous, he makes strategic decisions with his head, not his heart, and he is patient.[15]) The Templars, God rest their souls, paid the price for that at Hattin, at the same time that we were driving south through Panasium. But that, of course, was a year after the disaster at Myriocephalon.

Emboldened by Nureddin's death, and Saladin's concentration on Syria, Kilidj once again attacked the Danishmends, and two of *their* princes appeared in Constantinople seeking succour from the Emperor. One of them, called Shahinshah, was actually Arslan's brother or half-brother. (I suppose that shouldn't really surprise either one of us, unfortunately.) The other one's name I cannot recall with certainty, only that it was difficult to write or pronounce.[16] Also, Arslan had seized cities and fortresses in the eastern part of the region of Cappadocia that the Empire claimed not only by virtue of ancient right, but also by an older agreement with Nureddin, in which that Sultan had promised to hand them over to Manuel after their reconquest, in return for Manuel not supporting Arslan against him.

Child's play to follow so far, is it not?

I am relating all of these things because I want you to understand that the reasons for setting out on such an ambitious — and risky, because huge campaigns are always risky — campaign were sound. All treaties and breaches thereof aside, the Emperor was both responding to a very real threat, and trying to take advantage of a significant opportunity.

Saladin's disinterest (at least for the time being) in Anatolia was actually double-edged for Kilidj Arslan. While it prevented him from attacking Kilidj in defence of the Danishmends, it also very likely would prevent him from coming to his aid against any attack by the Romans. So if there was ever a good time to strike against Kilidj, this was it. Also, if Kilidj were to be completely successful in his efforts against the Danishmends, he would have been master of all of eastern and central Anatolia, as well as a powerful presence in the west, and thus a threat to Imperial possessions in that area, as well as the (very important) ports all down the western Anatolian coast.

And if Kilidj achieved *that*, it would only whet his appetite for further expansion at the expense of any or all of his neighbors. The Empire simply could not allow this; Kilidj had to either be subdued, or at least kept neutral in the region's growing power struggles.

Forget not, sister, that as a personal bodyguard, my ears have been privy to many conversations that even some of Manuel's highest officials have not — indeed, sometimes those very worthies were themselves the subjects of discussion. (And by the by, I take considerable pride in that the Emperor did *not* remove me from that position once it had become apparent that I was becoming proficient in Greek. He — the Emperor of the Romans — trusted *me*, a sword for hire from the farthest reaches of Christendom.)[17]

And Manuel saw that obnoxious lout Barbarossa as being an equal, or even greater threat than Arslan, especially because an alliance between the two was (and is) hardly unimaginable.

Barbarossa's designs on the East in general, and quite likely the Roman Empire in particular, are no secret. He has been actively seeking an ally or allies in Asia or Outremer, and not merely among Christians, either — and the Crusaders in Jerusalem and Palestine already acknowledge him as a benefactor and protector. The Romans believe he has also approached Saladin, and it would hardly surprise us if he suddenly found common interests with Arslan. In fact, Manuel was willing to wager (as were most of his advisors) that *Kilidj* [Arslan] had already made opening overtures to the German king.

If you are asking yourself how this paladin of Christendom could possibly bear arms alongside the Hagarene against fellow Christians, I shall furnish you with two reasons, the second most important one first. Any westerner who wishes to malign (or outright attack) the Romans can always fall back on their being "schismatics" who refuse to recognize the Bishop of Old Rome as the head of all Christians everywhere.[18] But the first and most important is that Barbarossa would make common cause with Satan himself if he thought it would increase his territories by a hairsbreadth or his treasury by half a copper.

Nor was this project undertaken on the spur of the moment. Arslan well knew the Emperor's intentions. We had undertaken the refortification of Dorylaeum and Sublaeum the previous year (and Manuel took part personally, as I have told you) before retiring to the City[19] for the winter. The Emperor was also able (in spite of Barbarossa's efforts) to maintain good relations with most of Outremer, as I will relate shortly. He had previously even married his niece to the Prince of Antioch.[20] Not surprisingly, then, Arslan sent an embassy to Constantinople, with offers to renew the old treaties. Manuel, knowing how much attention Kilidj had paid to those same treaties in the past, rejected their proposals.

Instead, he began comprehensive preparations for a campaign that would put a permanent end to this threat, and, if successful, restore Roman glory of old in what had once been the Empire's true heartlands, in central and western Anatolia.[21] Arslan had reneged on his promises for the last time; Manuel planned to ride right up to the very walls of Iconium itself, and take the Sultan's capital by force if he did not surrender it willingly. The Emperor swore that in either case, he intended to use the Sultan's back as a footstool when he [Arslan] prostrated himself to plead for mercy.

To this end, Manuel not only gathered as many warriors as possible to his banner, but also put his military craftsmen to work that entire winter in the construction of the implements of siege warfare — *ballistae, mangonels*, scaling ladders, and the like.[22]

Also the securing of vast quantities of lumber, hides, ropes and other materials vital to the investment of a large city, as well as the draft animals and wagons to transport them.[23] Troops were assembled from every possible quarter, and from every ally who could be relied upon, including the Kingdom of Jerusalem itself, sent by its young king Baldwin[24]. Also present was Baldwin of Antioch, the Emperor's brother-in-law[25], one of many noble and gallant men who did not return alive from that accursed pass.

Yet as ambitious — but I stress again, well thought-out — as Manuel's plans were, we were dogged by ill-fortune right from the beginning. Here, sister, I do not use the word "outset", because the delay of that very thing —actually just setting out in the first place — was itself the first major problem.

The Hungarians and Serbs were bound by numerous oaths and treaties to answer the Emperor's call to arms (his mother the Empress Irene had been a Hungarian princess!), but, for no reason I am aware of, they did not arrive at the assigned staging point in time for the campaign to set out in the spring, as planned. Instead, we found ourselves marching across Anatolia in the heat of late summer, much as the first Crusaders had done — against the advice of the Emperor Alexius, Manuel's grandfather — some eighty years ago on their way to Jerusalem.

But, I know you ask yourself, did they not take Jerusalem and Antioch from the infidels? What is my brother telling me? I am telling you that maybe only one man out of every five made it *to* those cities, and then very nearly died of thirst outside their walls.[26]

Yet those contingents were very important to the Emperor, and he wanted to proceed with the maximum force available to him. But perhaps he should have gone on without them. (As it turned out, we actually *did* go on without them, as most of them, when they did arrive, were assigned to the secondary force commanded by Andronicus Vatatzes, which I will get to in a moment.) But we all make our best decisions in hindsight, do we not?

So much also then for the omens that the Emperor had failed to heed, and which had predicted our disaster. Of course, the first I heard of any of these was on that grim return march past the heaps of mutilated bodies of both friend and foe, the sight of which still lingers somehow before my eyes, awake or asleep.

Word went through the ranks that one of the civilians, an interpreter attached to the contingent of [friendly] Turks (who, properly, and in keeping with longstanding agreements, marched on the Roman side), had gone to pray at a church dedicated to a certain Saint Cyrus on the morning before our departure. Only on the return march did it come to light that this man had apparently heard an icon of the Virgin cry out in fear for the Emperor's safety, wailing that neither Saint George nor Saint Theodore would be able to hold the Emperor back from his disastrous course.[27]

Later yet, I was told that Manuel had unwisely ignored a prophetic dream that had come to him shortly after he had first conceived of this campaign. He had apparently dreamt that he was on a warship on the Propontis [the Sea of Marmara] when the sky suddenly turned black, and the mountains of both Europe and Asia began to fall into the sea to crush him and his shipmates. I, who, as I have already related, have stood guard in the most intimate of the Imperial quarters, had never heard of these nightmares until after the battle. There were plenty of them then. For all of us.

Not one among us returned to Constantinople without having lost someone dear to their heart. For us, in the Guard, it was our oath and battle-brothers, but for the Romans it was in many cases blood relations. Nor were these losses respectful of rank or nobility, but were shared by all from the lowest-ranking footsoldier right up to the Emperor himself, whose own Imperial kinsmen were cut down in his very sight.

This was not a battle of the sort where unarmoured peasants with scythes and billing-hooks are slaughtered in their hundreds while knights ride around challenging each other to single combats, as though war was some kind of game.

I crave your pardon again, dear sister, as I suppose I keep going a little farther afield than I need to. I have picked up the quill again after a couple of cups of wine and a few hours' sleep. I shall strive to proceed more directly now; it is just that, as I have said already, reading history has taught me that nothing can be truly understood without an investigation of its causes, that is to say, what came before it.[28]

It also hasn't escaped me that I may well be protracting this simply because it may be my last opportunity to communicate with you for some time. I will miss you — and Henry — sorely. So, then.

Having mustered at Lopadion on the Rhyndakos, and with the northern contingents finally arrived and all of our supplies in place, we at last set out; quite simply, the most enormous force that at least any of us Varangians had ever seen.

Here I should note that the Emperor (and a number of his more seasoned officers) strongly considered waiting a few more weeks for cooler weather. But his younger — and less experienced — kinsmen had waited long enough already, at least as they saw it, and were eager for battle. (They needn't have worried, they were going to get it.) But I cannot really say that marching then was truly a rash decision; keeping that many men and animals in one place would have necessitated requisitioning almost every spare scrap of food up and down the Anatolian coastline. It probably just couldn't have been done.

So we began to march south, but not before the Emperor detached a small part of the gathered force under the command of Andronicus Vatatzes, and that Danishmend prince whose name I still can't remember[29] to secure the latter's claims at Neocaesaria. (As I mentioned earlier, this force in fact contained the better part of the Hungarians and Serbs whom we had spent forever awaiting.) Some believed this to have been a diversionary attack, hoping to draw off significant Turkish forces from our line of march, but that is unlikely. In fact, I find it difficult to even *imagine* what it would have taken to divert attention from an army that was transporting three thousand wagons of equipment. It was not as though we were going to take anybody by surprise! They probably could have heard us coming in Egypt.

For my own part, I believe the move was political, the Emperor hoping to gain support from Arslan's foes amongst his fellow Hagarenes. Also, it did *maybe* ease a *very* little bit of the supply problem, but that alone cannot have been the reason, especially not after waiting so long for their very arrival.

So we marched in the heat for almost four hundred miles, which took considerable time, as we had to rest frequently, and also constantly water the horses, mules, and oxen, which, as you well know, require even more to drink than does a man.

Then, at a place called Laodicea, we turned our faces east, and — apparently, someone told me, following the same path as the famed Macedonian Alexander[30] — marched for the interior of Anatolia.

The march until then had been arduous, but our real trials only began when we shortly crossed into what was (at least nominally) Turkish-held territory. The population there is sparse, mostly herdsman and their flocks, living in a manner similar to the various races of barbarians who have plagued the south Russian steppes from time immemorial.[31] Like them, these nomads are not to be dismissed lightly in time of war, and are regularly recruited into service (with promises of plunder) by the sultans they are — at least nominally — subject to. They fight primarily as mounted archers, and *very* dangerous ones. They are called Turkmen, or Turkomans. Why, I have no idea, other than that while generally of the same race, they are somehow distinct and separate from the Turks of the Sultanate.

But I do know that they serve as very effective marchwardens.[32] As soon as we passed into Turkish territory, there was little or no forage for us. There were light but persistent skirmishes between our scouts and the Turkmen as we moved forward, and they retreated, but not before laying waste to everything in our path. Not only had any crops been razed, but they also burned the very grass so that our animals had nothing to graze upon, and had to be fed out of supplies we had carried with us. Of course, we had anticipated this, and so were able to continue, but certainly not in comfort. And until we came to the wooded hills, a pall of smoke hung constantly over everything for miles, reducing visibility, and choking both man and beast. (And greatly increasing our thirst, which was again, of course, the enemy's intention.) The sun's presence was known only from its sweltering heat; for days and nights we saw not it nor moon nor stars as any more than faint ghosts through a haze of ashes.

And water very quickly became a problem, and had to be rationed strictly. Streams could not be depended upon — most of them were just dry beds at this time of year anyway — and the enemy had poisoned almost every well.[33] And when I say "almost" rather than "all", I mean exactly that, for that is the cruelty of these heathens.[34] Once our men, at least some of the less disciplined ones, knew of this, their thirst drove them to taking chances that this or that well might be pure, with the expected grievous results. And another thing, too: I cannot tell you how it weighed upon the spirits of the rest of us to pass wells, our throats burning for water, *knowing* that there was a chance that theirs was harmless, and indeed, life-sustaining.

Their tactics had the desired effect. As careful as most of us tried to be, and try as we might to restrict ourselves to the water we had brought casks of with us in wagon after wagon and loaded on mules, as well as whatever we could still bring up our supply line, a deadly sickness tore through our ranks.

Whether its direct cause really was fouled water, or some other of the likes that sometimes baffle our physicians and other learned men alike, I cannot say, only that it was a vicious bowel flux that struck down both man and beast. Cramps so severe that they doubled strong men over as though they had been hit in the stomach with cudgels, and you will forgive my directness, but constant, sudden, and uncontrollable urges to relieve one's bowels. Myself, I was fortunate, or blessed, to have suffered only mildly in comparison. I was only afflicted for four days or so, and was always able to make the latrine when in camp, or at least somewhere off to the side of the line of march when we were moving. Many others could not. Also, unlike many less fortunate men, I was able to keep food down, and thus at least keep up my strength somewhat. (Not that I had much appetite amongst those sights, and even worse, those smells, or that there was any abundance of provisions anyway.)

Others, though, suffered this "bloody flux" to the point that they were unable to walk without assistance; some began to rave, having become delirious with fever, and not a few died, of what I can only describe as shitting (and sometimes vomiting) their lives out. Faecal matter was shot through with blood and a loathsome-looking type of pus, accompanied by far too much — and often bloody — fluid.

Nor, as I said, did it spare the beasts, who of course simply relieved themselves where they stood, sometimes in what looked like an impossibly constant flow. We were at all times besieged by our own shit, probably diseased shit. (It has always struck me how the weavers of the epic tales and poems seem to have forgotten *these* aspects of war.) The Emperor himself was not affected by this physically — or if he was, it was mild enough for him to successfully conceal it — but he was sorely grieved by the suffering around him, and looking back, it might have been at this time that his mood began to truly darken. Himself having some knowledge of the physician's art, he told us that the men who were succumbing were, in essence, dying of thirst.[35]

Again, I crave your pardon, but this is what we lived through, and still carried on. We marched in good military order, appropriate to the terrain we were crossing. The route was scouted at least a day's march ahead, despite constant harassment from the Turkmen skirmishers. (Being with the Emperor, I of course had no part of that particular action, and nor did any other

Varangian, but we did hear that it was even more than usually savage.) Our scouts though, may God bless them, got the better of those fights, putting the Sultan's irregulars to flight every time, and keeping our main force safe from their attacks.

Each night, we camped in the proper and time-honoured Roman manner, fortified and entrenched, with pickets and constant perimeter patrols. Not even at our sickest did we lose our discipline with regard to these matters of military science, that the Romans have known since before the Nativity of Our Lord to be essential not only to an army's success, but to its very survival.

All of which makes subsequent events all the more difficult to explain. But I will come to that.

While the flux was at its worst, we kept our daily marches short, despite our decreasing provisions, in order to rest both men and animals. Many of the latter that were too sick or too weak to continue were put out of their misery. This eased our provision problem slightly, although many men, while hungry, were reluctant to partake of the meat of a diseased animal. Myself, I believe the Emperor was correct when he assured us that their illness — like our own — was concentrated in their digestive tracts, not their flesh. But I myself took none of it. While I would love to say that it was because others needed meat more than I did, I have promised complete honesty with no embellishment. My appetite was such that I could barely stomach my normal bread rations, but forced them down to maintain my strength.[36]

And over that week, we also dug a great many graves. The physicians certainly had their hands full, but neither were the chaplains idle. I remember thinking at that time that I was fortunate to be a soldier, despite the many horrors that mine eyes had already seen over the years, and that it was well that I had not been given over to the Church, for to have to minister so to the dead and dying would have broken me. I do not exaggerate, sister, for I feel the moisture building in my eyes even as I write this. I swear to you on Henry's soul and my own that, aside from not being an ordained clergyman, I could give last rites or conduct a burial service — in Greek — from memory.

And so we marched, we *soldiers*, until we came to a place called Myriocephalon, may God curse its name and its very stones until the Final Judgement and beyond. And there again, we built an entrenched marching camp, properly fortified and guarded, just as we had each and every night before, despite our illness and our hunger, because that is what *soldiers* do. It is not only the press of battle that they shrink not from; they also neither desert nor mutiny because their supplies run low, or it gets too hot, or too cold, or rains too much.[37]

And it was to that camp that Kilidj Arslan sent an embassy, seeking peace.

The last day's march had been a very short one, intentionally so, in order to allow for a good rest before the morrow. Ideally, we might have camped an extra day or two, but with disease still present (although to a much lesser extent; but it had done most of its damage already), remaining in place very long might not have been prudent. Renewed outbreak was not a fanciful concern, not to mention our provisioning problem. Our intention was to spend the night in camp, and then march — or force — our way through the Tziviritze Pass, which now lay before us, and that I suppose the old ruin of Myriocephalon had guarded in some past age. From there, it would, if unopposed, have been a solid day's march, even at our speed, to the walls of Iconium.

Apparently, the Sultan's peace proposal amounted to little more than offering to renew the earlier treaties that had been broken time and again. Manuel gave the envoys a polite audience, as he never failed to do, but, after brief conference with his senior officers, rejected their proposals in their entirety, and dismissed them.

The officers were by no means all in agreement during that short council. The Emperor's detractors have since been eager to report that he largely ignored the advice of battle-scarred grey-bearded generals who had fought and won many a campaign for him before, in both Europe and Asia, and instead gave ear to his younger relatives. Men whose personal valour and skill of arms were not, and are not, in question, but who had little or no campaign experience. In short, the impetuous youth raised on the heroic tales of old, who lust for the glory of battle right up until they've actually been in one. Sadly — and though their courage did not falter in the press — the morrow's battle would be the only one many of them would ever fight, as that cursed pass would drink its fill of their blood.

Having been standing guard in a position where I was able to hear clearly all of the arguments and opinions myself, I think that this is a little unfair to the Emperor. Yes, the opinions for and against did mostly — but not completely — fall along the lines of age, but one must consider what kind of emperor Manuel was. *He was a soldier-emperor*, and by no means a young one, with scars and grey hairs aplenty.[38] He knew that both sides had valid points, but that *he* had to make the ultimate decision.

On the one hand, we had been considerably weakened by the dysentery outbreak. We were going into steep, rugged, enemy-held territory full of the kinds of narrow ravines and defiles that are an ambusher's delight.

But on the other, our force was still the biggest army an emperor had put in the field since before Manuel's grandfather's[39] day. We still had all of our siege equipment. The time and expense that had gone into mustering this force would be very difficult to repeat, should the Sultan not keep his promises — the very same ones that he had never kept before. If that was all that was on offer, we had already come too far, and sacrificed too much to turn around now.

I actually believed, as did the Emperor, and many officers both old and young, that the real purpose of the embassy was to reconnoitre our camp, and get an up-close look at what condition we were in after all of the privations they had forced upon us. A tactic as old as war, but one the Emperor felt no need to counter. There was no need to even blindfold[40] them, we had no objection to their seeing that our strength was still very likely up to the intended task.

And so we spent our last night in camp, trying to get as much rest as possible. But as you know, there is often very little sleep on the night before battle. Some men *do* sleep somehow, sometimes by seeking their comfort in the arms of those few women who somehow always manage to follow an army, even into enemy territory. Others spend the better part of the night in prayer, or in raucous banter with their comrades. (I have always heard that few civilians can comprehend that men who beard and insult one another in such manner around the campfire, are the same ones who will gladly die shoulder-to-shoulder with these same men — their battle-brothers — the very next day.) Myself, like many others, I *try* to get some sleep, but mostly end up just inspecting and sharpening the same weapons a dozen times over.

We weren't even sure that there *would* be battle on any scale the next day. They might try to attack us in the pass, but did we not have scouts and skirmishers to prevent that? (We did, but it turned out for some reason that I cannot to this day comprehend, that we did not use them, or at least not properly. Or at least *some* of our leaders didn't. I will recount the sorry tale, and *you* be the judge.)

We thought that they (especially with all of their light-horse archers), would most likely try to engage us on the plain after we emerged on the other side of the pass, and turned south towards Iconium. Stopping us would have been unlikely, but they could have hoped to inflict heavy losses. The kind that would have told over time with us encamped before Iconium, with those same light horse harassing a very long and vulnerable supply line.

But why, when we did everything else right, did we neglect to properly scout the pass ahead of us, particularly the heights above it? Even considering the risk of remaining in place another day, a scouting patrol in force could have cleared those heights of ambushers.

This is territory with which the enemy, particularly the Turkmen, are very familiar. And the Turkmen, unlike most other nomadic horse-tribes, are not reluctant to dismount and fight as infantry should the terrain require it. That type of fighting, although not what they are most suited to and favoured of, is by no means alien to them. Thus they were not completely out of their element deploying themselves on foot amongst the wooded slopes that towered directly over our intended line of march. And more of them were flocking to Kilidj's banner daily. Another day in camp meant another day's worth of reinforcements for the enemy, and another day's worth of losses for us to the aforementioned bowel disease, which was not yet done with us. And as I said, there were some amongst us who feared it might actually get worse again if we remained in place.

Also, even if a fairly strong force of infantry dislodged the Turks, they would then have to have held those slopes against inevitable Turkish counterattacks throughout the night. For my own part, I believe our men — particularly when you reckon with what it was they actually accomplished that day — would have held their position. But they would also have had to pass a night without sleep or probably food, straight into a second consecutive day of hard fighting to keep holding off the enemy while the rest of us passed through the defiles. And *we* would have come out the other side straight into the jaws of the enemy, with no friendly-held point to rally to. Actually having had such a point was one of the main things that, by the grace of God , saved us.

The Emperor's decision then, was to press ahead, and to force the passes that day. The sooner we began to entrench ourselves outside Iconium, the better.

But nor did we just blindly march into a trap, as many (most of whom were never anywhere near Myriocephalon or the Tzivirítze Pass, as this place is called) would have you believe.

We were acutely aware of the nature of the terrain that we had to pass through. It was essentially a series of connecting ravines — to even call them "valleys" would be wildly inaccurate — that varied from narrow to narrower. To the north were the wooded mountain slopes that we were most concerned with, but the southern borders of these ravines were also marked by an almost, but not quite, unbroken line of low hills that ensured an enemy could have advantage of us from both flanks. The southern slopes of those hills were steep cliffs, falling off into even deeper gorges. And worse (as it turned out), these hills, as I said, did *not* form a continuous line; there were places where our right flank would be bordered by sheer drops that spelled certain death for any man or beast who took but one step too far to the right.

Obviously, the terrain dictated that our line of march be thinner and more compressed than we would have preferred. In fact, I have been told, and have no reason to doubt, that by the time we had fully entered the pass, our line stretched out over ten miles.

I have also heard suggestions that Manuel should have set aside the baggage-train and its attendants until the main part of the army was through and we securely held the pass. But those who suggest that seem to forget that we were already well into hostile Seljuk territory, and all that equipment would have to have been left in a heavily-guarded camp, which would have meant splitting our force. Also, there could then have been a chance of the enemy bypassing our main force by using the heights, and, instead of attacking us — I say "us" because I presume I would have been marching through the ravines with the Emperor — attacking the camp and quite possibly burning or even capturing all of the siege-equipment. Once again, that would have rendered the entire expedition pointless; we *had* to get that gear to Iconium. That city's walls were not going to fall for us like Jericho's did for Joshua.[41]

That was why it had been placed in the middle of our line of march, where we had hoped it would be the safest. But that, too, turned out to be a major part of our undoing.

So in the morning we broke camp [September 17], and marched out in good order, in a formation long-recommended by the many Roman generals who have set down their wisdom and experience in books for those who, in turn, have the wisdom to read them. The weather, although still uncomfortably warm, did not yet threaten in any way.

If I recall the details correctly, and I am certain that I do, the vanguard (wisely) consisted primarily of infantry, and was commanded by the brothers John and Andronicus Angelus. They were followed closely by the main body of the army, consisting of the eastern and western *tagma*[42] troops, the backbone of any Imperial field army, commanded by Constantine Makrodoukas and Andronicus Lapardos. Following them came the Latin contingent, which, along with some other troops, formed our right wing under the Emperor's nephew Baldwin.[43] Then came the enormous baggage-train, with all of its oxen, wagons, equipment, supplies, and attendants. These were followed by our left wing, which largely consisted of our less experienced troops and freshest recruits (hence the decision to place them into what was thought to be a position of relative safety).[44]

Next came the Emperor's own contingent, including myself, your brother, amongst his Varangians, and very close to his side. With us rode the *kataphraktoi*, the Roman heavy cavalry, as a kind of a reserve to be deployed to a crisis point, or (God forbid) help us Varangians defend the Emperor if it came to it. Also, the Emperor's chief nobles and advisors, including the generals, usually had bodyguards and household troops of their own. (I should just say as an aside, dear sister, that although none of those gave me actual reason in my own experience to distrust them, I never liked having them around, at least not too close, because of all the stories of court betrayals that we always heard. We of the Guard had our own secret standing order that no Roman officer had ever given us, not even the *hetaireiarch* — whenever any of these grandees was accompanied by his private bodyguards in the Emperor's presence, we matched them at least one-to-one or better, regardless of what the regular duty postings were. I think that Manuel knew, and that our loyalty brought at least some little joy to his heart.)

Finally, came the rearguard, consisting of seasoned troops under Andronicus Kontostephanos, who, as I will relate, was the light that rallied us when our lamp burned its lowest, and even the Emperor seemed on the verge of despair.

Now sister, you surely understand that an army of the size I have described is really, in a sense, only nominally under the command of one leader — the one who makes the biggest decisions, such as when to attempt the pass, in our case. But how those decisions are carried out by the various contingents that make up the army depend upon the officers the supreme commander has entrusted with them, and indeed, the abilities of the even more junior officers within them.

If that sounds like I am leading up to blaming somebody in particular, I assure you upon our mother's soul that I am not. No one person or commander is or was solely responsible for what followed.

The vanguard, commanded as I have said by the Angelus brothers, was the first to enter the pass. While I was (literally) miles away from that action, I was close enough to the Emperor to be privy to all of the reports coming in through runners, flag signals, and the like.

The vanguard executed its appointed task perfectly. Well, I suppose I should say *almost* perfectly, as perfection does not exist in war, at least not in the face of the enemy. Not only did they lead us into the pass, but also, very much like the reconnaissance in force I have discussed earlier, fanned out hard to their left [north] flank, with their heaviest [most well-armoured] infantry challenging the Turkmen for the string of hills that formed the bottom part of the northern slopes. It was from these positions that the enemy had hoped to rain missiles [arrows, javelins, shots from slings, and even rolling boulders] down onto us.

But the Angelus brothers had studied their *tactica* well. The lighter-armed archers, protected by other light infantrymen with shields, were able to both move forward and exchange our own "darts" (as some of the Greek writers love to call arrows) with the Turkmen, despite the latter being in better natural cover. This would have been accomplished by advancing in sections; that is to say, one section would aim and shoot a volley of arrows, the arc of its flight being high enough for friendly troops to pass under. The other section marched forward, double-time, and then took up shooting positions, while the first shooters prepared to take their turn to advance in the same manner.

No doubt our Roman arrows were intended less to kill the enemy on the spot as to root them *to* the spot; to keep their heads down, and prevent them from leaving the rocky outcrops that they were sheltering behind. The idea would have been to keep their attention fixed on the threat in front of and below them, rather than the one approaching from *their* right flank.

In this way, our heavy infantrymen were able to reach and engage the Turkmen, no doubt using time-honoured Roman shield-formations to protect themselves while covering the intervening ground, and being supported by the archers in the ravine.

Once they reached the Turkmen's positions, there was no contest as to who would hold the lower hills; it took only a short time to put the enemy to flight, and in a disorderly manner. Our men, I am told, maintained good professional soldierly discipline, and kept formation as they pressed further up the northern slopes in pursuit, right up to the treeline that marks the beginning of the woods that cover the higher mountainsides.

The Angelus brothers forbade their men to pursue the enemy into the woods. It would have been far too dangerous to do so, as the woods were doubtless well-known to the Turkmen, giving them ample opportunities for ambush. Also, it would have delayed the advance.

And so the vanguard marched onward, through the ravines, and also along the lower slopes to the north of them. They were harried with ambush attempts all along the way, but fought their way through each of them. The reason for this is simple, but critical. By the use of their heavy infantry, the brother-generals had denied the Turkmen the positions on the lower slopes that were within a good bowshot's range of our troops marching below.

The problem was that we didn't maintain control of those slopes long enough for the *entire* army to march through. The eastern and western *tagma*, the "main body", which would have formed the centre if the army was arrayed for battle on an open field, instead of being stretched out in a line ten miles long, commanded, as I said, by Constantine Makrodoukas and Andronicus Lapardos, followed next. They too were able to negotiate the pass with only very moderate losses, as they followed hard on the heels of the vanguard, with almost no space between the two sections of the army. They patrolled their flanks in the same manner as the vanguard had, and thus prevented the enemy from filtering back down into the ambush positions they so coveted.

In fact — and this is probably the biggest thing that, by the grace of God, saved us from complete and utter destruction — the vanguard under the (thrice-blessed) Angelus brothers forced their way through to the far end of the pass, where they found a hill that was a little higher and more isolated from the majority of the others. They immediately took control of it, and began to construct a strongly-fortified marching-camp (again in the tried and tested Roman manner) even while under ceaseless harassment from the Turkish archers. No doubt there must have been constant duels between the bowmen of both armies, and the men labouring to build the camp would have been doing so whilst ever harking for the whisper of the unpredictable shaft about to impale them from out of nowhere.

For my own part, I find it harder even than most to stomach that kind of situation, so my heart truly goes out to those men. That isn't to say that I hadn't ever been in it — nor wouldn't later that same day — but I much prefer the fight face-to-face, hand-to-hand. That is where your training, your skill, your experience, and aye, your valour and that of the men beside you tell. But sometimes there is not much defence against a stray arrow. We all remember King Harold, do we not?[45] I know many a man who shrugs this off, saying that an arrow will only find him if God has deemed it to be his time. But for me, I have spent all my life training for war, and pray that I do not blaspheme in saying that it dismays me when pure stupid luck (or bad luck) triumphs over hard-won skill.

So anyway, as I said, the *tagmatic* troops were hard on the heels of the van, and so reached the campsite being established, and were able to assist in its construction and defence.

Had everything continued in this manner, the Emperor would have been master of Iconium today.

But of course, it obviously did not.

The next section was the right wing, composed primarily of Latins, and led by the Emperor's nephew Baldwin, a valiant warrior and respected commander.

Once again, dear sister, I remind you that I am not writing this to place blame on anyone or any contingent in particular, so please consider my words carefully, as I mean them precisely as I write them. Please do not charge me with attempting to lay blame at Baldwin's feet.

As I have already related, the vanguard had cleared the lower slopes of enemy ambushers, and the *tagmatic* troops who immediately followed them pushed through in much the same way, both infantry and cavalry. But they merely passed through on their way to — correctly — seizing and fortifying a position for the rest of the army to rally to on the other side of the pass. They did not leave men behind to maintain control of those lower slopes. They probably expected the following contingents to proceed through (expeditiously) in the same manner as they had, and also would have been loath to dilute their own force, knowing that the main Seljuk body was awaiting them at the other end of the pass. I don't think they were mistaken in any of this.

But Baldwin, the commander of the right wing, which was based around the heavily-armoured Latin cavalry of Jerusalem and Antioch, did not follow Makrodoukas and Lapardos directly, and allowed a considerable gap to form in our line.

Again, I stress that I am not accusing him of stupidity, only inexperience with the Turk, and particularly the Turkmen. He no doubt had valid reasons in his own mind for not closing that gap. He may have thought that, with a primarily cavalry force, he would have been able to make up distance very quickly, and thus that allowing a gap to form would not be as critical as it would have had more of his troops been on foot. Most likely though, he was perhaps overly cognizant of the baggage-train being right behind him, and was afraid that if he got too far ahead of it, the enemy might then slip into a gap *behind* him, and strike at our all-important siege -gear. I think he held he held back to ensure the safety of the baggage-train.

We could ask him, if he or any of his men were still alive.

But this was probably the opportunity the enemy had been waiting for, at least since they realized that they couldn't stop us from the front, or at least stop a good part of our force from getting through to the other side.

It was the baggage-train that they had to stop at all costs, and both sides knew that.

It also probably didn't help brave young Baldwin that he was leading cavalry through terrain where infantry reigns supreme. Even if he had wanted to maintain control of the slopes, he didn't have nearly enough footsoldiers to do it, and even if he had dismounted some of his horsemen, they wouldn't have known how to prosecute that kind of fight properly.

In that kind of terrain, the cavalry's main task is simply to pass through it alive, in order to fight on a battlefield more suited to their strengths. And to pray.

So the Turks not only returned to their former ambush positions, but also, through their intimate knowledge of the environs (and a gap they could sneak through by their half-hidden paths without our archers being able to see them), were able to take up positions on the crags to our right.

They had now apparently decided to press their attack from the sides and rear. From what I heard, too, they were significantly reinforced by more Turkmen while they allowed us to commit most of our army into the pass before they sprung their next trap. And why would we not have committed? It was all or nothing, by the grace of God, at this point.

Not wishing, as I said, to move forward too quickly and leave the slow-moving but all-important baggage-train unprotected from its front, Baldwin permitted the Turks to reclaim the ambush positions they had previously held, without much opposition, if any at all. The Turks did, I am told, move stealthily, so it is possible that he did not realize the full peril of his position until it was too late.

That would likely have been because the Turks did not begin to shoot their arrows, and hurl their javelins and rocks until we were right where they wanted us. And they were in position all along the heights now, to both flanks of our force, including that gods-damned baggage-train. The heights that we had given them command of without any fight — saving the initial one when our fearless vanguard had cleared them off.

When they began to attack, Baldwin probably realized that there were more of them, and closer than he had thought. In his defence, perhaps he had assumed that the initial engagement with the vanguard had bloodied them more than it had, and therefore underestimated their strength.

Or maybe he sat his horse, sick to his stomach, knowing that the enemy were completely filling the space he had to pass through, but knowing also that if he moved forward to engage them, then the other Turks on the heights above the baggage-train would be able to swoop down on it unopposed. (The pass at this point was so narrow as to make it impossible to put even a single solid file of troops on either side of the train.)

It may only have been when the enemy began to shoot that the truly dire nature of the situation became fully clear. Heavy volleys coming down from both sides threw Baldwin's formations into disarray; he was unable to form up to defend against only one side, although I imagine that the heaviest concentration of missiles came from the north, on the left flank. (Actually, I don't have to *imagine* anything; I would very shortly find myself in a similar situation.)

Baldwin tried to rally his troops in front of the wagons, but without success, and the Turks, having no doubt hoped for this disorder, spilled down from the heights onto his contingent under cover of their ceaseless volleys. Thus the Turkish infantry, armed with spear, shield, and saber were able to charge in and engage the Latin men-at-arms.[46]

Worse still, the Turkish foot came at Baldwin's men not from two, but three sides. Scores of them swept down into the ravine itself in order to attack directly from the front, obviously in no fear of exposing their own rear to the *tagmatic* troops, who had already passed too far ahead to be able to turn back to support the right wing. Even had they still been close enough to try, they might not have been able to get through, because of the enemy's possession of the high ground (that they themselves had originally cleared of that same enemy).

Now Baldwin was being pressed not only from the sides, but back against the baggage-train.

And now the Turks began their attacks in earnest all down our line. The left wing, behind the baggage-train and in front of my own [the Emperor's] contingent was pressed sorely by flights of arrows from both sides. Our archers, of course, tried to respond, but were far fewer in number than those of the Turks, and were quickly overwhelmed. (Most of our bowmen had been with the vanguard, and were already through the pass.) The left wing contained most of our least-experienced troops, many of them recruited only shortly before this campaign. It hurts me to say, but panic became a factor.

The baggage-train, with its three thousand wagons, and thousands more draft and pack animals, could no longer move forward. Of course, this had been the lynchpin of the enemy's strategy all along.

The Turks who remained on the heights now concentrated their fury on the baggage-train, and its animals and drovers. The vast majority of those men were not trained soldiers, but servants attached to the army to handle the masses of beasts and equipment. Also, some of the siege-specialists whose areas of expertise were the mangonels, the preparation of Greek Fire[47], and the like, were not soldiers who otherwise marched in the line.

Animals were slaughtered, bucking and braying to escape their harnesses, and their handlers were pierced by arrows or crushed by the bouncing boulders that the Turks mercilessly rolled down the slopes. Others were kicked to death or trampled by the very beasts that they had cared for for months, or even years. We had had some archers stationed in some of the wagons, but they were few, and though by the Holy Cross, they acquitted themselves boldly, they were swiftly marked and eliminated by the Turks. The sound alone of that awful slaughter of man and beast, as it carried to me through the ravines, is something I shall never forget or escape, awake or asleep.

Nor the smell. Anyone who has ever been to war knows it has a smell, the stink of blood and shit and fear. Sometimes other things, too, especially depending how much is on fire, or if the battle lasts days, and there are rotting corpses spread in every direction. But this was even worse somehow, at least in the moment, even from the distance I was still at.

Maybe it was because even before the rout — and rout it was

— of the baggage-train, many of the animals (and men, too) were still suffering from the flux, and were still relieving their bowels anywhere they could. Maybe it was just that, along with the usual carpet of offal that covers any battlefield, concentrated as it was by the narrowness of the ravine.

But for me, and more importantly, I think also for Emperor Manuel, it was not only the stink of slaughter, but also of certain defeat. Now I am no poet, but I know what we heard, smelled, and saw in those moments. We *knew* that the dream of Imperial — of *Christian* — reconquest of Anatolia was dying in that dust that was quickly becoming a sea of mud — composed of blood, entrails, and worse.

The animals and drovers lost to us, none of that siege-equipment was going anywhere, and it became very obvious, in a matter of moments really, that our only remaining objective was to extricate an army sufficiently intact to fight another day.

We also heard the pitiful cries of those trying to escape the carnage amongst the wagons, but they had nowhere to escape *to*. The merciless Turks were to either side of them, to the north and south. To their front, the east, Baldwin and his men were beset on three sides, with their backs pressed hard against that self-same doomed baggage-train. Some of the surviving drovers and others who had accompanied the wagons tried to turn back, fleeing into the ranks of the left wing behind them, causing many of the greenest troops to fall into confusion, and in many cases, that truly worst nightmare of any commander, even further panic.

Any refuge they would have found would have been but the cruel delusion of a moment's duration, for as I have related, the Turks had already begun to attack the entire line, and the left wing suffered badly.

The enemy's true plan had come to fruition, probably better than they had dared to hope even in their accursed heathen dreams. Our precious siege-train was now a useless — and immovable — obstacle, cutting our army in half. The front couldn't retreat, and the rear couldn't advance to support the front. And now the rear, too, was under attack from both sides.

Us too. I was now in the fight.

You may be wondering why the Turks didn't try to set the siege-train alight with fire-arrows. Had you been there, though, you would have seen the profusion of dry grasses and shrubs that extended throughout the ravine, and really all the way up to the treeline. Any fire would have swiftly gotten out of control and gone wild, posing as much of a threat to the Turks as to us. Also, they may have had designs on capturing some of the gear — as they certainly had on the valuables — but I am sure that that was a secondary consideration beside the real peril of a fire in that locale.

The last report I heard before my attention naturally shrank to the Emperor, myself, and our immediate environs was not encouraging, but nonetheless worthy not only of relation, but of deathless recollection.

Young Baldwin, the Emperor's nephew, had seen that he was pressed and hemmed in on all sides, without hope of relief. His men-at-arms were being cut and shot down on all sides, though they spilled heathen blood in equal measure and more as they fell. Knowing, no doubt, that defending was hopeless, he wagered all on the greatest weapon of the Latins; gathering all the knights of his household, and all the other mounted men that he had, for one last, desperate, all-or-nothing cavalry charge. The charge of the western chivalry that had carried all before it on so many battlefields in the past.

Ordering his footsoldiers to open a path, Baldwin of Antioch, nephew to the Roman Emperor Manuel Comnenus, spurred his steel-clad destrier forward at the head of his men, the banners and pennants of Antioch, Jerusalem, and many noble others flying from their lances, and the din of battle itself momentarily overwhelmed by the old Crusader battle-cry of "Christ and the Holy Sepulchre!"

And the lines of Turks did shudder and bend, but there were simply too many of them to break. And the God-cursed terrain was against the Latins, as they tried to charge uphill to scatter the Turks who were doing the most damage to our army.

I later heard that Baldwin and his personal escort punched hundreds of yards into the Turkish mass, a highway of vengeance for what was being done to our men. But they were too few, and before long, the last of them was seen to be pulled down into the roiling sea of Turks, no doubt to be torn to pieces.

I also have no doubt that not a single heathen who was present — and actually survived — ever forgot that charge.

But that same angry sea then closed in over the path those brave knights had carved, and surged against the remaining Antiochene infantrymen, who died fighting on their feet, to the last man.

At this point, of course, progress forward had ground to a halt. As the Turks pressed in on our division, we formed up around the Emperor, the Roman *kataphraktoi* trying to give us infantrymen some protection with their shields, the newer, larger ones which Providence had seen fit to inspire the Emperor to equip them with only recently.[48]

There was no way to withstand the Turks as we were, and indeed, as soon as they identified the Emperor's position, they concentrated their attacks on us. A more poetic man might say that their arrows and javelins darkened the sky, which would be an exaggeration, but I can tell you that they were the heaviest flights *I* have ever seen, and I have seen many.

A decision had to be made, and it had to be made quickly, without conference or council. Keep in mind that some of what I have related is based upon reports I heard *after* the battle; despite our signals and runners, we were by no means in possession of a complete picture of what was going on past the disaster directly in front of us. We knew that the vanguard and *tagmatic* troops had punched through and had been trying to hold a hill as a rallying point, but had heard nothing more (that *I* knew of) for some time.

I am always amazed by those who compare battles or even wars to games of draughts.[49] The only way a game of draughts could be like a battle would be if you played a version in which you didn't always know where all of your own pieces were, much less those of your opponent, and even when it was your turn, your pieces didn't (or couldn't) always do what you wanted them to.

Manuel had to decide whether or not to try to retreat back out of the ravine, not being certain of whether Kontostephanos and the rearguard would be able to provide support, or whether they too were now engaged, and if so, how heavily. (This was not due to any failing on the part of Kontostephanos, his force had been deliberately held back a little farther, to act as a kind of reserve, but the sheer ferocity of the Turks' attack cut off all communication, so we may have mistakenly allowed too much of a gap.) The alternative was to try to press forward through the wreckage of the baggage-train, as well as the body of the enemy, to try to join whatever forces he had remaining on the other side.

It was at that very moment that the Hagarenes struck another terrible blow to our hearts. Above us on the heights, in full sight of almost all — for by this point, the survivors of the baggage-train, the left wing, and the force I was in were close to having merged into one — a Turk raised up a gruesome trophy, calling everyone's attention to it. There, at the end of a long lance, was skewered the head of another Imperial nephew, Andronicus Vatatzes, still recognizable to his kinsmen despite its battered state.

Thus the infidels informed us of the fate of the force sent against Amasia, which many on both sides were no doubt certain we would now share.

The Turks' tactic was particularly effective on the greenest recruits in the left wing, who had already been thrown into considerable disarray from having the survivors of the baggage-train (as well as some loose animals) running straight into them. Many,

I am sad to say, threw down their weapons and tried to run — and in their confusion, not even all towards the rear — running into and tripping over one another, and some (who had kept their weapons) even striking each other down in their haste to attain I know not what imagined safety. All they obtained was a quicker death by Turkish dart.

Although the officers of the left had completely lost control of their formation, the more hardened troops, led by their *decurions* and other lower-ranking leaders[50], formed a line that the would-be deserters could not break through. Somehow, by the grace of God, shouted orders, fists, and the flats of sword-blades, they were able to stem the tide.

Perhaps also the realization (if they were still even capable of coherent thought at that point) that even if they got through *that* line, they would then have to get through *us*.

There were doubtless many who now called to mind the omens (if, as I said before, there had *actually* been any) and were certain that God had abandoned us to our fates, but the Emperor was not yet one of them.

Our chances of besieging Iconium were utterly lost, but Manuel still had an army to think of. Retreat *might* have been possible, but if the vanguard and the *tagmae* had really gotten through to a defensible rallying point, then all that their valour would have earned them would have been the opportunity to be completely cut off and surrounded in enemy territory, with their only options being death or capture. Unless *we* reinforced them. The army's only realistic chance for survival was to reunite it, even if that was on the far side of the pass.

And here I risk stating the obvious, but I feel I must, as it pertains to my main reason for writing this letter. Retreat, as uncertain of success as it might have been, would probably have been the option that would have given Manuel the better odds of ensuring *his own* escape and survival. But the Emperor put the survival of his men above simply saving his own skin at any cost. He had led us here, he was going to lead us out.

So Manuel decided we had to rally our troops and push through. We began to march forward in close formation, getting as much protection from our shields as possible. Orders were sent forward to the remains of the left wing to form up on us as we approached, and that we were going to force our way through the wreckage of the baggage-train.

But as we approached, although the better part of the troops ahead of us fell into formation, others did not, especially as the weight of Turkish missiles that they faced only increased with proximity to the Emperor. Yet now they fled in the opposite direction, almost as though in obedience to the orders to move forward, but in truth they were attempting to flee the greatest fury of the Turkish onslaught. They did so in complete disorder, and I believe there were even some amongst that crowd who desired to link up and stand with the Emperor, but were borne along to their doom by the reckless tide of their fellows.

We would be picking our way through their bodies soon.

Yet we may in part owe our own survival to the other troops in the left wing, and the veterans who brought them back into order. Advancing ahead of us in proper Roman formation, they cut their way through the Turks who were already flooding into the pass to fill the gap between us and the baggage-train. But unfortunately, as I understand it, when they actually reached that barrier, the Turks were able to turn them to the right, into a smaller ravine that seemed to promise escape (or at least away around), but in fact only turned back sharply into the main ravine, and an ambush that slaughtered them almost to a man.

Dreadful as this further loss of comrades was, word of it brought back to us by the ragged handful of survivors who managed to escape to warn us, only made it more plain that our only way was straight through.

Also, their bravery had allowed us to close the gap; we had now come to the hell-on-earth that had only hours ago been the hope of conquering a city and a kingdom, and now lay deserted, in a ruined shambles.

It was the worst scene I have laid eyes upon on any battlefield, and the next hours were the worst I have ever gone through, mind, body, and soul. Many of those who had not yet thought that God had deserted us did now, in the face of that awful carnage.

But none of the remaining soldiers desired to flee.

Yet there still remained some noncombatants who had somehow managed not to perish amongst the beasts and wagons. Many of them were wounded, and even more stumbled about like walking corpses. They were not soldiers, and their terror had gone past the point of hysteria, which was perhaps fortunate for them, because most of those whose hadn't had run straight into the Turks' arrows or onto their spears.

There was little we could do for them where we were (unless we wanted to surrender ourselves, which was out of the question). But their fate was not something the Emperor took lightly. I could see the grief and the sorrow on his sweat-stained face as he put out the word that they were released from their duties, and free to try to save themselves in any way they thought fit. If they tried to flee to the west, north, or south, they would not be considered deserters, and were to repeat the Emperor's words to that effect, should they somehow run into the rearguard. Any Imperial slaves were manumitted[51] on the spot.

The Emperor addressed them quickly but calmly, thanking them for their service up to this point, and advising them that they had only three real choices. First, to attempt flight, and he even recommended that if that was their choice, then they should try to separate, as a man alone might have a better chance than in a group, especially if he could make it into the trees. Second was to wait until we had moved on, and surrender to the mercy of the Turks. Third, to arm themselves as best they could, and follow us.

I am sad to say that very few indeed took the third option, but nor can I entirely blame them.

We pressed forward, harried from both flanks by the Turks.

There are some on the Roman side (who weren't there) who would tell you that Manuel now led us in a desperate and glorious charge through the infidels to safety, which is completely ridiculous. There *was* a charge, later, but at this point, it was only by the grace of God that we could stay on our feet.

We entered the bloody morass, and began to pick our way through the abandoned wagons, discarded equipment, and the bodies of men and animals, many crushed beyond recognition. And all the blood and bile and piss and shit had transformed the dust and dirt on the ground into a sucking putrescence that I swear tried with some diabolical will of its own to hold down our boots and transfix us to the spot in order to make us easier to slaughter.

The heat had become unbearable, particularly in the crowded confines, and not only parched our throats, but magnified the stench of spilled entrails all around us, and legions of flies were already well into their customary feast. War always gifts them, and carrion birds by the hundred were seen circling overhead, the whole breadth of the sky.

We were gagging, wrapping whatever scraps of cloth we could tear off anything over our mouths and noses, and many a hard man vomited, but did so on the march.

The cavalrymen dismounted, leading their horses beside them to our flanks, trusting to slung shields and the heavy barding[52] of the *kataphraktoi*'s mounts to protect their beloved animals. In battle, I am an infantryman, and when I ride, it is for transportation. But I do know that the bond between these men and their steeds was such that it made them sick at heart to use them as living shields in this manner. But choice we had none.

In the midst of armoured horses and upraised shields, we tried to find a path forward, knowing that our only hope lay in extricating ourselves from this Satan's maze.

But arrows still came through, and from all sides. And men fell. A few of our men who had bows — very few, most of whom were not professional archers, but had managed to pick them up from the dead — tried to send some arrows back, but they had to shoot high and blind, and so probably did little damage.[53]

You asked me of my own wounds, though they were but trifling compared to those of others. An arrow grazed me on the side of my neck, just as I was turning my head at one point; I suppose that the chainmail that hung from my helmet (precisely to protect the back and sides of my neck!) must have snagged on something and allowed just this tiny space that the Devil permitted an arrow to be in at that precise instant. It only grazed me and stung quite a bit, but I thought little of it at the time, only to thank God that it hadn't been an inch or two to the right, and thus through my throat. It was only well after the battle that it was discovered that the God-cursed Turkish shaft had left a tiny, filthy splinter that caused the wound to fester. It then had to be cut out and drained, leaving the scar you saw, which is much bigger than the mark originally left by the arrow.

I was blessed that that was the only arrow that hit me at that point. At least most of us were well-armoured, and many of the enemy's shafts were reduced to wounding, rather than killing. But there was no way we could withstand this at the pace we were making for much longer. (And I should also never forget special prayers of thanksgiving for the trainers of those warhorses, who held up through this at least as steadily as we men did.)

There was no way we were going to get through by winding our way around every obstacle. Many of the wagons had been crushed by stones rolled down from above, but others had just been abandoned in place, fully loaded, upright and relatively undamaged. We would have to turn obstacles into shelter.

As we reached them, we began to heave the wagons that had lost parts of their heavy loads over onto their sides, propping them up with whatever was to hand. Others we had to quickly hurl the burdens from, in order to be able to flip them with sheer muscle power. All of this was done under constant assault from the Turks; men with shields trying to protect those lifting the barricades past which the men behind them would hasten forward to throw up more wagons wherever possible, again with some men covering, some men clearing and heaving. We did this to face what we perceived as the greater threat from the north, while we now concentrated the horse-barrier to the south.

I have to emphasize, because it is after all my stated purpose in writing this letter, that the Emperor was shoulder-to-shoulder with us in all of this, both raising obstacles into place and protecting others who were. In fact, I have it on reliable authority that another of my fellow Guardsmen inspected the Emperor's shield after the battle, and found it to have been struck by no less than thirty arrows over the course of that day.

Despite our best efforts, we couldn't construct an unbroken barricade. (I should mention at this point too that part of the reason that we were going to these efforts was to clear a straight path through the wreckage, so that, *if* we still had a rearguard somewhere behind us, it might be able to overtake and reinforce us more easily.) The Turks took full advantage of the gaps to attack us directly, trying to use the makeshift protective barriers we had erected against us as blind spots to get close.

And close they did get, trying at least half a dozen times to break our line, which would have spelled certain death for all of us. But they were thrown back every time, by sword, axe, and shield — and by that I mean smashing shields into snarling faces so close to your own that you could smell their stinking breath. The spear got less use, the fighting was now so close, and our lines so thin. I struck more than once with my sword's pommel, with no room to swing or stab. (I lost my axe early on in the melee; it stuck in something — or preferably *someone* — and was wrenched away from me.)

The savagery of the Turks in those gaps was such that they

struck not only with their weapons, but their bare hands, one pushing another into us in their frenzy to drag us down by sheer force of numbers. But hold we did, and I know that, at least in those moments, none could deny that God and Michael[54], as well as St. Demetrius and both Theodores were with us. One of the younger, wilder Danes even later claimed that he had seen Odin, but of course he was mistaken.

I would have thought that if anyone had any vision out of the old religions, it would have been of the Valkyries coming to choose the dead. But there would hardly have been room for them, the sky was becoming so black with crows.

I nearly got my hand crushed in this fight, which surely would have prevented me from surviving the rest of the day. We were shoulder-to-shoulder, and the man to my left staggered back, stunned by a rock. Before we could close the gap, a wild-haired Turk with no helmet, who was literally frothing at the mouth like a rabid dog, leapt at me from my left, but just as he would have been upon me, I met him with an uppercut-type blow with the rim of my shield. I was able to get most of my weight behind it, and it stopped and stunned him, and may well have broken his jaw.

Then just as suddenly, his brains were leaking all over my shield-arm. One of the stones hurled from above by his fellow Turks had landed square on his unprotected head, and then bounced inside my shield, which I had not yet been able to withdraw. It didn't hit square, and my hand was of course protected by a leather and steel-reinforced gauntlet. But one of my shield's handle-straps was ripped free, and my top finger took enough impact to numb it and start it immediately swelling. And the cursed rock bounced again, up (because of the angle of the inside of my shield, no doubt) and struck me again in the left shoulder, not hard enough by now to injure it seriously — especially not through the padding beneath my chainmail[55] — but enough to also numb it momentarily. Which would have been all the next Turk, who was stepping right onto his fallen comrade's body to get at me and finish me, would have needed. But at that instant, even as I tried to raise my dangling shield, the man to my left who had been stunned was already stepping back into the fight, and split my assailant's face right down the middle with an axe.

Before I could say or do anything, I was hauled back out of the front line by a rough and powerful hand on my right shoulder, whose owner shoved me back and stepped forward to take my place in the line. It was none less than John Kantakuzenos, another of the Emperor's close relations and highest-ranking officers. Unfortunately, later that day, I would not be in a position to return the favour, and he was yet another noble warrior who was lost to us and to the Imperial family.

When I say every man fought shoulder-to-shoulder, I mean it. No one stood watching this nightmare from the safety of some far-off hill. At least not anyone who fought on our side.

I passed my shield to another man who had lost his, but could still make use of my damaged one, and discarded my gauntlet before swelling made it impossible to do so. I sheathed my sword and lent my strength where it was needed to hold up the ruined wagons-turned-barricades.

And not a heartbeat too soon. I ran — along with five or six others — to where we saw a mass of Turks swarming one of the heavier wagons, even climbing up on one another's shoulders in order to overturn it on our men who were desperately trying to hold it up and avoid being crushed. There were gaps to either side of the wagon, but they were filled with dead animals and men, as well as discarded cargo. But if the Turks overpowered the defenders (who I saw included the *hetaireiarch* himself), they would have a bridge right over their broken bodies into our midst.

As I ran, I saw one Turk rising up to where his thighs were above the top edge of the wood (the devil must have climbed up over two of his comrades' shoulders), with a spear that he was about to start stabbing down into our men with. There being nothing else to hand, I grabbed a fist-sized rock off the ground with my uninjured right hand and threw.

It was an easy target at fifteen paces, and caught him by surprise, in the stomach. It probably did no harm, but it hit him just as he had been drawing back to strike, and he stumbled, losing his balance, and fell back over into his companions. I don't recall seeing him again, but in the heat of battle, that means nothing.

As I rushed to assist the *hetaireiarch* and his comrades, a couple of our men who had secured some of the heavy wooden yokes used to harness the oxen slammed them up against our side for reinforcement. It helped, but it was only a matter of seconds before the back ends of these supports were digging furrows in the mud as the Turks inexorably forced the wagon over. It was past its centre-point, and coming down on us. We knew that if we couldn't hold it, the men closest would have had no chance to escape.

But then, just when I thought my lungs would burst, we heard shrieks of agony from the other side. The force opposing us dissipated almost completely, and so quickly that some of us (myself included) lost our footing as the wagon went crashing over the *other* way, onto the Turks.

We were able to form up defensively to repel any attempt at crossing this suddenly-appearing bridge, but they did not attempt it, the obstacle being too high. It had fallen towards them, with a considerable number of their bodies under it, forming a shoulder-height barrier on their side. And, to their credit, they applied themselves to trying to pull any survivors out from underneath it.

I only heard later how God's grace had spared us yet again. While we were struggling to keep from being crushed, some others of our men had found that one of the wagons abandoned nearby had contained a cargo of extra *menavlion* spears, the super-heavy (and extra-long) spears the elite Roman infantrymen use to set against enemy charges. The kind that, set and held properly (usually by a crew where two men brace and guide the spear, while a third provides shield-protection) can spit an armoured horse end to end. These men had taken three of these, and, working together, had somehow crept through the bodies in the gap to our left, and surprised the enemy with hard, two-man thrusts of these fearsome weapons, ending their bid to crush us and swarm into our line.

As I said, at that point in the battle at least, the saints were with us. This was not the only close brush with disaster that we had; I later heard of many others. But even during that struggle, more of our men were able to get past behind us, on our way through this obstacle course, the like of which I could never have imagined above the regions of Hell itself.

But on we pressed, albeit knowing that even more Turks were waiting at the end of it. I myself did no more fighting in the ruins of the baggage-train; I wouldn't have been much use in the front without a shield, and even in the spots where there might have been room, being in the second or third rank as a spearman has never been my lot. For those last minutes — that seemed hours — I was employed in helping to move our wounded forward. Some leaned on me for support as they limped along as fast as they could, and carried a shield to cover the both of us. Others, who could not walk, we lashed to broken boards (which were very plentiful) that we used as stretchers.

I recall one lad, so young his beard was only starting to grow in properly, who must have been one of that handful of remaining archers I spoke of. Most of his right leg and part of his left was smashed to pieces, and there was no doubt that he would lose both even if we got out alive. Yet he had still retained his bow, and though his quiver was gone, he clutched a fistful of Turkish arrows he had collected, and, although tears of agony covered his filthy face, he loosed those bolts one by one over the heads of our defenders even as we carried him on a board, until he had no more, and only then passed out.

He was just a "little Greek".

We were getting the wounded onto horses or mules, whether they were cavalrymen or not, sometimes two to an animal. Once we broke out of the wreckage, we were going to have to move fast, and we didn't want to leave anyone behind to be taken by the Turks.

We did not yet know that anyone who fell there would remain there; we would never retrieve any of our fallen comrades to bring them home.

And suddenly, like that, we reached what had been the front of our baggage-train. Which is not to say that the way forward lay unobstructed. The ravine ahead was littered with the bodies of Baldwin's men who had died fighting to protect that very baggage-train, and those of the enemy that they had taken with them.

The Emperor, whom I was very near again, we having regained some semblance of normal order and formation at this rallying-point (if you could call it that), gave further orders. There was something of a lull at this point, as the Turks pulled back slightly, planning to re-engage us as we struggled through the open in the ravine. Had there not been, I might not have been able to make out his words; his normally powerful voice was reduced by thirst and dust and heat and fatigue to a hoarse croak from shouting commands in the melee. The pounding in my own ears and head — like the others, I needed water badly — didn't help.

And we had no more water. The last we had had, we had given to the wounded.

Again, the Emperor told us, the way out was straight through, and the cavalry would be in the front, with him in personal command. Over the protests of myself and the other Varangians, Manuel chose a few of his best *kataphraktoi* to act temporarily as his personal guard, whereas we would accompany and bolster the other remaining infantry. We would march double-time to keep as close pace to the cavalry as possible, and also be responsible for the remaining horses and the wounded.

Our protests fell silent as we saw that his plan, though fraught with risk, was our best option. And it was not, dear sister, as unworkable as it sounds. Except in rare circumstances, the

Roman heavy cavalry advance is more of a fast canter than a headlong charge, the emphasis not being so much on the speed of the individual horses and riders, as on all of them hitting the enemy's front line at the same instant. I once heard a cavalry officer say that it was not meant to be an avalanche of steel, but rather a solid wall. As we only had a short distance to cover to engage the enemy directly in front of us, the gap between cavalry and infantry would not at any point be very great, and possible to close quickly, before any Turks could pour in from the flanks to divide us.

The cavalry, spearheaded by the Emperor himself, would form the hard, sharp point of a long, narrow "V", the two sides of which would consist of us infantrymen, some (including myself) leading horses with the vulnerable wounded in the middle of the two lines, with a handful of archers who could still sit a horse and shoot. I was on the right (south) side of the line now, so I could have my sword arm free towards any enemies from that side; I held a mare's bridle in my injured left. Strapped to her back was an unconscious man who seemed to be barely gurgling for breath, black blood trickling from his mouth and gathering in his matted beard, occasionally dripping to the ground below. You would have expected the blood to be mixed with saliva, but he probably had none left. None of us did.

I wish I had known his name, for his life was in my hands. And God forgive me, I would fail him.

The order was given to advance, and we did so, double-time, the Emperor and the heavy cavalry striking into the Turkish lines and — God be praised — throwing them into disarray. (To be fair to Arslan's regular army, I should probably admit here that it may have been to our good fortune that the majority of those who opposed us right there were the less disciplined Turkman tribesmen.)

I led the mare, trying to keep her in step and as calm as I could, and a close comrade of mine, also a Saxon, whose name was Aethelnoth, marched to the outside of us, trying to provide as much protection with his shield as possible. Myself, I wasn't much use at this point in the fight; I would have done better to have strapped a shield to my right arm for extra protection, if I could have found another intact one. As it was, I had found one that was only moderately damaged, and hung it over the right side of the horse to help cover the wounded man.

My sword was not a useful weapon at that moment, as there were no Turks that close to me. That would change.

We pushed ahead quickly, and probably made a good half-mile at that pace, the Turks falling back before our advance, but again pressing our line harder from the flanks as it lengthened.

Their seemingly endless supply of arrows came down on us constantly, but no longer in disciplined volleys — more like a heavy rainstorm that goes in fits and starts. Those who had shields kept an eye overhead, and those of us who did not put our faith in God and our brothers who did, and simply kept moving forward. If God had decided that an arrow would find me, or a weak place in my armour, it would find me, if not, then not. (And no, dear sister, I have not forgotten what I said earlier on this subject! There was just nothing else I could do about it.) My mail *was* grazed at least twice, and the slung shield stopped three more.

Twice the Turks pressed in close enough that I had to brace Aethelnoth's back to help prevent them from breaking through, although it was spears from behind us that threw back the infidels; my own attempts to stab one-handed over the top met nothing. I only tried two or three times anyway; it was too awkward while bracing Aethelnoth and still holding the mare's reigns.

As you can imagine, the press and squeeze of bodies was awful, especially in that heat, wearing armour and having had no water since early morning. And the Turks now increasing their pressure as they did only made it hotter and tighter. All of us were fighting to breathe, and it felt almost like there was not enough air, putrid as it was, to go around. I am certain many of the wounded expired at that time without us even realizing it.

When I think about it — which is every bloody day — I pray that my man did, because I think it would have been a far more merciful end for him than had he still been drawing breath during what happened next.

We were coming to a widening of the ravine, but also a break in the line of hills to the south (our right and my side of the line). The ground dropped off sharply in places where we were suddenly walking along the edges of a series of steep cliffs. To describe it as broken terrain would be an understatement.

But this was the part that, the enemy knew, if we passed through, we would be out of the worst part of their trap.

So perhaps there was now some desperation on their part, because if our army got through, although we might not have been able to take Iconium, we could have done a lot of damage to the Sultan's heartlands.

They came at us now without restraint, holding nothing and no one back, from three sides.

And just as we braced for another snarling wave of Turkish infantry to break over us, some devil — or perhaps one of their *djinn* — chose to play his bloody game with all of us, Christian and heathen alike.

Out of nowhere, and taking scant minutes to gather its full force, a violent wind whipped up, carrying with it the sand and grit of that season's parched earth. Day became night, and worse than night; there was not a man who was not choked and blinded by the flying grit, and animals that were already skittish, edged quickly towards panic.

So as that wave of Turks, undeterred in their ferocity by the storm, struck us, seen only as shadows rearing up out of the murk, I was unable this time to aid Aethelnoth or any other of my battle-brothers, as the mare whose reigns I held whinnied in fright, and pulled hard, as though to rear. I sheathed my sword and tried to use all my little knowledge of horses to stroke her, talk to her (though I had to do my best to shout to be heard above the wind and all the other dreadful noise of battle) to calm her, but it was to no avail.

I was deathly afraid that she would throw the wounded man from her back to be trampled, despite the ties securing him. As she began to run ahead blindly, snorting in terror —I knew I would have seen her frothing at the mouth and rolling her eyes had the storm allowed me to see any more than the vague shape of her head — I tried to stay with her, attempting in vain to steady her.

My world collapsed to her and me. My last glimpse of Aethelnoth was of him engaged with two Turks at once, and then I only saw flashes of struggling here and there as we passed, like in a dream. The howling of the wind even deadened some of the screaming.

We must have gone about twenty or thirty yards when the horse suddenly lost her footing, lurching forward and down. She must have stepped over one of the narrow crevasses that now bedeviled the southern flank of our position, into thin air. Yet there must have been some slope, because I could hear her hooves scrabbling for purchase on the shale, which was being kicked up at me. I tried to pull her back, but suddenly she was over the edge, neighing and whinnying and kicking. She must have gone end over end, because I was now flat on the ground, my already injured left hand grasping the bridle for all I was worth, with my left shoulder feeling as though it had been — or was about to be — pulled out of its socket.

I knew the mare was still partially supported by the slope (or something); there was no way I could be holding her up on my own. But I was being inexorably pulled to the edge, and prone as I was, I couldn't get my right hand to reach the bridle-rope. And I didn't dare scramble up, because that would only have jeopardized whatever counterweight I was providing. I was praying desperately for help from someone, anyone, in case the man tied to that horse was still alive.

But it was not to be.

As my fist clutching the bridle-rope came inches from the edge, a darker shadow quickly passed over me, and all the weight was gone. When I felt the remaining bit of bridle-rope that I still held in my fingers — for a visual inspection would have been difficult — I found that it had not torn, but been cut clean. Whether by friend or foe, in mercy or in malice, I know not.

I can hardly describe the things that happened next, nor do I particularly wish to, for not only do the memories cause me pain, but so do the questions that I ask myself every day and night, and yet never get closer to answering.

Did I kill any friends? Did I kill fellow Christians? Did I kill fellow Romans?

I had gotten to my knees in that blistering cloud of pestilence — for the wind also bore the stench of death, and more than a few flies — and was trying to get my bearings. I had been pulled along and rolled on the ground, but I thought I could still be sure of the direction I was facing, although beyond about two feet from my face I could make out no more than vague shapes.

I drew my sword and began to rise, and was instantly hit from behind on my left side and sent sprawling. It had to have been a running horse, because I heard it snorting after it hit me, but I had heard no warning hoofbeats in the howling wind and dust. But it was only a glancing blow, so the horse had not been coming straight at me, or perhaps had had a rider who had turned it at the last instant. So, again by the grace of God, I was not trampled, and nothing was broken. Neither had I lost my sword, for I had slipped my wrist through the leather thong attached to its pommel (for this very reason), even though my hand had opened and I might have lost it otherwise.

But I definitely had had the wind knocked out of me, and surely my ribs were bruised. But as I said, I wasn't spitting blood that wasn't only from my cut lips, so probably nothing was bleeding inside. I got up to a knee again, but this time I was less certain of my direction. Fortunately, squinting upwards, I was able to make out a pinprick of slightly brighter yellow-brown that had to be the sun, and turned myself what I thought was forward. My face was wrapped in cloth below my helmet, and I could barely breathe or see, but I had to keep moving, for all three of duty, honour, and survival.

Shapes of man and beast flashed this way and that, like images cast by a shadow-lantern, here one instant and gone the next. Some were fleeing, some were fighting, some I know not what.

Friend and foe were indistinguishable in that maelstrom, and all order of any kind had broken down. Beasts trampled men, and men struck out at beasts to fend them off, often only maddening them further. Romans and Turks, three-quarters sightless, ran into, and in many cases fell over one another. Many in their terror struck out at whoever was before them, lest they strike first. Many more fell blindly into the gorges, as had the mare I had been trying to lead. And the man I had been trying to save.

I know of these things not only from my own experience, but from all I heard later. I was actually lucky (again!) to have been on the right flank, because further to the left the press of bodies was such that some could only move by stabbing and hacking like butchers at whatever impeded them, in many cases not even having enough room to properly swing. Men pushed others over cliffsides without knowing, seemingly without caring whether they were sworn foes or brothers-in-arms of a dozen years. And by some devil's trick, even though we could hear no orders, nor even make out the words of a man arm's-length away, the wind brought us the echoes of the screams of those who fell. Any who lost their footing were trampled and suffocated.

At least, by God's grace, there was some room to move in my vicinity, although there were, as I said, random clashes of arms all around me, everyone against everyone, and every man for himself.

I have to stop to take a gulp of wine to steady my stomach before I go on, this still sickens me so.

For my own part, and I thank God and His saints for this daily, I was able to restrain myself from that kind of blind panic, and struck at none who did not strike at me. I just kept trying to move *forward*, according to the last orders I had been given.

But the fighting found me, and I had to defend myself at least a half-dozen times. Mostly it was just someone trying to run past or through me, and I was able to disengage or push off quickly, but there was at least one man I had to put down (and probably killed), and another that I am sure I at least injured severely. Stout as your heart is, I will give no more details on this part, for as I said earlier, I am terrified, and indeed sickened at the very possibility that I may have killed battle-brothers, whether defending myself or not.

As far as further injury to myself went, blades bit through twice to (again) my left shoulder, but not too deeply. I have suffered battle-injuries before, but never so many all to precisely the same part of my body, as though it had been some type of magnet for the enemy's weapons.

Almost as suddenly as it had come up, the windstorm abated, letting the dust settle on a scene that an icon painter who regularly portrayed the torments of sinners in Hell would have shrunk from.

Bodies, parts of bodies, and piles of guts separated from their owners lay strewn about in every direction. I have seen the aftermath of battle, the fields and plains of massacre, but never like that. There weren't just *bodies*, but *piles*, where they had fallen upon one another in their confusion and terror. The gullies and ditches they had stumbled into were filled with them.

And God help me, but the piles were still moving in places. There were injured men half-buried among the dead — and I am certain that there were men who had been buried alive completely amongst them, and had either suffocated, or had literally drowned in the flowing blood and gore of others before it merged with the dust that was everywhere, producing a gritty paste that coated and got into everything.

Some were only partially buried, probably hiding wounds that did not allow them to free themselves, in other cases only a head or a filthy arm could be seen. And these wretched souls were calling — *croaking*, really, was all that they could manage — for succour from their comrades, from anyone.

But their pleas went ignored.

Perhaps it was we who still stood who, in those icons, were not the unfortunate damned, but the imps who tormented them. For despite all the horror already wrought, we fought on.

I suppose I could say that the lust or frenzy of battle was upon us all, but that would be a lie. It was not on me, and I was sickened by the spectacle. Yet I, too, did nothing but move on.

Caring nothing for their own wounded, the Turks' only thought was to continue to pursue the Romans. It was probably as much from the desire to strip booty from corpses (some were already ransacking the baggage-train behind us), as it was from any desire to defeat us Christians utterly. The Turkmen bands had always flocked to the Sultan's banner primarily at the promise of spoils, and in this case they were not disappointed.

Nonetheless, they were coming for us, so we in our turn could only keep moving past those who reached out for, and cried out to us as we hurried past, no doubt thinking us the most heartless monsters ever born, and cursing us to eternity with their dying breaths as we moved on, taking all hope with us.

And here I must confess yet another shameful act of my own. Knowing I could not stop, I did my best not to look at the faces of the pleading men, nor to listen too closely to the dust-choked, croaking voices.

Lest I recognized any of them.

And please understand, I *knew* I couldn't stop to help, and not just because of the danger to myself, but because I had a duty to the Emperor. We had been ordered to move *forward*, and with all possible speed, that being the *army's* only chance of survival.

I did not then know the whereabouts of the Emperor (whose sworn bodyguard please recall I was), nor whether he had gotten through, or if so, how far. Or whether he was even still alive. But my first duty was to him and my orders from him.

Or maybe that's just a coward's excuse that I'm passing off as duty. I think I did not the *right* thing, but the thing that *had* to be done. I suppose I am burdening you with this in the hope that you can somehow forgive me in the stead of unnumbered who cannot, but I know that is just a vain hope on my part. Born of the desperation of endless nightmares.

Please also know that it *did* cross my mind to try to find some officers to make an attempt to rally our troops around to form a cordon which we could use to rescue at least some of those trapped men. But it was very clear that there wouldn't be enough of us, and would almost certainly have resulted in the rescuers being lost as well, lost to the Emperor, who probably needed every last fighting-man he still had. At least that's what I tell myself, night after night.

So I moved forward through the carnage, leaving all in God's hands as to whether I would fall victim to one of the random Turkish arrows that were still falling amongst us. Having no shield, and doubting the reliability of my left side generally, particularly my shoulder and index finger (which had swollen up badly and I couldn't really move), I tore a strip of (relatively) clean cloth, and tied my dagger into my left hand as best I could. I could grip firmly with the bottom three fingers and the thumb, so I thought I could use it if need be, without just losing it. I have practiced fighting with two blades, and can hold my own, but it has never been my strong point; I am a sword (or axe) and shield man, and like to use my shield aggressively. And an off-hand[56] dagger is no protection against missiles.

One mercy was that the farther I got from the area where the dust-storm had been worst (apart from no longer hearing that terrible choir of pleading), was that the Turkmen's attack fell off somewhat, at least temporarily, as the tribesmen rushed to pillage the bodies and wagons. I shudder to think it, but I know this to be true: the only mercy received by those men whom we passed by was a cut throat before their bodies were despoiled, and worse. (Which I will yet relate.)

There were others like myself who had come through to a greater or lesser degree intact, and we gathered into groups as we tried to increase our speed. There were Varangians, Roman infantrymen, and unhorsed *kataphraktoi*, but we organized ourselves around the *decurions* and other junior officers present, along the lines of who had or didn't have shields, in order to give each group the best protection.

And so, still harassed by Turkish arrows, we marched, following in what we hoped were the Emperor's footsteps.

We made it, I would say, through about a half-mile or more of this broken desolation, strewn as it was with nearly two corpses for every boulder. But the respite, such as it was, did not last long. We soon heard sounds of fighting from just over the next rise, directly in front of us. It didn't sound like any vast group of men, but it did yet manage to give the impression of being close and desperate.

My group, consisting of less than twenty men, was first over the rise, and my heart leapt into my throat from both joy and terror, in equal mixture. There, on a small knoll topped by one of the few hardy trees that had been able to find purchase in this ravine (a wild pear, I think), was the Emperor! He and about another half-dozen Romans were circled up, their backs to the tree, with a couple of slain Turks at their feet, but at least two dozen more were pressing in on them.

As I rushed to their aid, the others with me, I heard the cry:

"Varyagi na Tsarya!"[57]

It was one of the old war cries of the Varangian Guard, that every member understood, though he had not another word of Russian.

I had charged headlong several more paces before I even realized that the command had come from my own throat, without regard to the units or ranks of anyone else present.

I never received any censure, then or later.

We had surprised the Turks, who were on foot, and we closed the distance quickly, crashing into a melee in which neither side had thought or time for formation.

There were slightly more of them, but we were now on both sides of them. My only thought was to cut my way through to Manuel's side.

The first Turk in my way was shieldless, like me, so I guess I was lucky. Again. He had a heavy scimitar that he brought down at a viscious angle, hoping to cut me from shoulder to hipbone. But I had that dagger lashed to my left hand, and as you know (having seen it years ago), it was blessed with considerable cross-hilts for turning or trapping enemy blades. I was able to catch enough of the blow to deflect it downwards, to rake harmlessly down the left side of my chainmail. His blow was powerful, though, and wrenched the dagger out of my hand, binding and all.

Instead of swinging or stabbing, I smashed my still-armoured right fist (while still holding my sword) straight into his face. He staggered back a step, spitting blood (and maybe teeth), which gave me the room to slam a right-footed heel kick into the middle of his chest while he was still slightly off-balance. He stumbled back further, and fell heavily, and though I didn't stop to finish him, I stomped down hard on his head on my way through.

I was just remotely aware of another scimitar missing me by inches somewhere behind me; if I hadn't kept moving, I probably would have been dead. As it was, I parried another blow from my right, and, locking blades at the hilt with this next Turk — who was smaller than me — I punched him in the kidneys with my now-free left hand, hitting with the bottom of my bare fist, and just pushed him off from me by overpowering him with my superior size and strength. Then I turned back forward just in time to parry another stabbing thrust at my face. I returned the favour, my blade still sliding back along my attacker's until I buried its point in his throat. I withdrew it in a gout of blood and gurgling as the Turk dropped his weapon, uselessly clutching his hands to his erupting throat as he lurched to his knees, dying.

I sidestepped again as I flicked the gore from my blade, and I was through.

John Kantakuzenos was there again, shielding the Emperor with his body, although there no longer appeared to be any need. The appearance and fury of our sudden attack had put the band of Turks — who doubtless hadn't been able to believe their luck, thinking that the Emperor was virtually alone and that they would easily capture or kill him — to flight in the direction whence we had come, leaving more than half their number dead or dying on the knoll.

We did not pursue; the Emperor was our priority, nor did we wish to rush back towards the Turkish arrows. In any event, those Turks' luck had reversed completely, as they were about to run straight into more Romans.

I went immediately to the Emperor's side, but he sat back down against the pear tree, a picture of exhaustion. He still held the broken remains of his shield, and a broken piece of a lance that he had been using at close quarters in the fight. He was filthy, sweaty, and battered like we all were, and I could see him bleeding from an as-yet unbandaged cut or stab wound to his instep. But worst of all, his helmet was badly dented, although still on, and I could see blood leaking down his face from some injury that was hidden by his loose hair and headgear.

Kantakuzenos quietly informed me and some of Manuel's

other closest personal guards that almost everyone in the lead had been separated during the worst part of the dust-storm, and even many of those who had survived had lost their mounts, often killed directly under them. Others, through misstep, had fallen to their deaths.

The Emperor, as I heard it, had been found alone on the knoll by a cavalryman who had lost his horse. He had been leaning against the pear tree — and some would later say that he had been resting in its shade — but it sounded more to me like he had collapsed against it. He had dismounted, and tied his horse up to the tree. His sword was lost, and he had no bodyguards until the cavalryman approached him. Apparently, his helmet had been knocked askew in the fighting, whenever it had been dented, probably by a mace or even a rock.

The story was then, and has since been told, that Manuel was for some reason unable to set his own helmet straight, and the other soldier helped him to do it. This is important, because this only makes sense to me in two possible ways, because Manuel didn't wear a helmet much different from mine, other than his having been adorned with a small gold cross. It was pretty much the same type of helmet any Saxon *housecarl*[58] would have been familiar with. The reinforced steel cap, the noseguard, the eyeguards, and a curtain of fine chainmail to protect the cheeks and the back of the neck. It didn't have to be intricately fitted into some other piece of a complicated suit of plate. So, and understand that I mean no disloyalty to the Emperor by saying this, unless it was the case that the cavalry-man had had to at least partially bang out the dent (which was still visible) to make it sit properly again, this tale shows that at some point, Manuel had suffered a severe blow to the head, and might still have been reeling from it somewhat.

He may have been found dizzy, or dazed, or fumbling with the chinstrap, but I know that he sustained a head blow at some point — that no doubt would have killed him *but* for his helmet — and from what little chance I had to observe him, he seemed even more ashen-faced than the rest of us. And again, we could not ask the cavalryman later, as he unfortunately left his bones not much farther on. But I believed then, and do now, that the blow could well have affected Manuel's behaviour later that day and the next.

Still, between the two of them, they had managed to kill a couple of Turks who had rushed them, hoping to steal Manuel's richly caparisoned horse, the Emperor having had only a broken lance for a weapon. They were then joined by the other three or four Romans that we first saw them with, but the other Turks had then immediately caught sight of them and made to surround them. Their plans, however, were foiled when we arrived on the scene.

We had little time before more of the heathens would be upon us, and we knew it. We had to keep moving, as did any more bands of survivors behind us, or we would be trapped when the Turks reorganized themselves.

Another dozen or so men hastened up to join us as we gathered weapons from the fallen to try to replace what we had lost. I found a kind of cross between a dagger and a shortsword that had a good hilt on it to carry in my left hand, and a small axe that I stuck in my belt. The Emperor, having replaced his own sword and heartened a little bit, was on the verge of giving us orders to march, when news from the men just arrived came to his ears of the Turks' wholesale plunder of the baggage-train. Not so interested in the siege-weapons, these (mostly Turkmen) had carried off the remaining food-supplies (which couldn't have amounted to much) and the considerable quantities of coin it had carried. Worst of all, someone had seen a Turk with an especially exquisite jeweled cross that had been commissioned specifically for the blessing of this expedition. And someone was unwise enough to mention it in the Emperor's hearing.

He looked again as though he had been physically struck. His eyes darted this way and that, as though trying to locate something, but not being sure where (or perhaps even what) it was. He was drawing breath rapidly, but with difficulty, as though he had just been running.

He began to give orders to go back to retake the remains of the baggage-train, but not with his customary authority, but rather a frantic tone none of us had heard him speak in before.

Every man knew that to do so would be suicide, not only for us, but for any other remaining elements of the Roman army, ahead of or behind us. Yet every one of us was oath- and duty-bound to the Emperor, and not only by the regular (and still sacred) ones that bind regular soldiers, but personal ones on top of those, and we would have gone with him where he commanded.

And I stress here, dear sister, that he was not simply ordering us to our deaths, but was planning to lead us there from the front. He seemed to have lost all sense of the severity — or perhaps *reality* — of the situation we were in.

But — and may that man take a seat at the right hand of Christ in Paradise — Kantakuzenos threw rank and precedence to the wind, and approached his Imperial kinsman, an armoured hand on an armoured shoulder, and gently pulled Manuel close, so they could speak quietly, face-to-face. As we others watched, it appeared to us that Kantakuzenos' words had a soothing effect, and Manuel nodded a couple of times, as though in agreement with what his officer was saying.

At last, Manuel nodded vigorously, and clapped Kantakuzenos on the shoulder, turning back to the rest of us, seeming, at least for a moment, his old self.

"The baggage-train and all our supplies are lost," he stated in the calm voice we were all accustomed to hearing, "but our brothers are not. The Hagarene and the Devil can throw dice over our trinkets, we move forward to reinforce the men of our vanguard, if they still survive!" A ragged cheer went up, the best our parched throats could muster, and the Emperor Manuel was saluted with raised weapons.

The Emperor remounted (stumbling just a little, I noticed). And so did any others who still had horses, which wasn't many. (I wouldn't have taken one even if there had been one available; without a shield, it would have just made me a bigger target.) While most of us moved forward around the Emperor, Kantakuzenos took a few still-mounted cavalrymen and followed us from some little distance as a kind of rearguard (Where in the hell was our *actual* rearguard?) that could still quickly rejoin us if necessary.

And so we moved on, through yet more desolation and death, until the broken ground no longer dropped off to the right, but instead provided *more* low hills, perfect for *more* ambushes.

We topped a rise, as warily as we were able in our ragged condition, and found, to the relief of our hearts and bodies, water. A fast-running stream came over the hill from the south-east, and crossed our path, but did not appear to be too bad of an obstacle, looking shallow enough to ford if we were careful.

We were already on the verge of becoming half-crazed with thirst, but the Emperor ordered us to cross before we stopped to drink, lest the enemy somehow come up behind us, despite Kantakuzenos' force.

We crossed in good order without incident, and maintaining our discipline, took turns at watching while others scooped water into their helmets and drank, also filling any waterskins we still had. The horses, too, were allowed to take their fill while their riders watched for the enemy. We were done quickly enough, each man knowing that to do any more than take the edge off his thirst would be to invite violent stomach cramps of the worst kind. We were experienced, disciplined soldiers.

And as badly as we needed water, the enemy knew it, too. This had every making of a trap. The watering-hole in the forest where all the animals come to drink, one eye looking over their shoulders for the predators surely lying in wait.

Suddenly the Emperor, sitting his horse and drinking from a

helmet that had been proffered him, violently cast the water away with a curse, his lips and hands trembling, ordering the rest of us to stop too, crying:

"How can we drink this water?! It is fouled with the blood of Christians! The blood of our comrades!" He began to spit, and cross himself at the same time.

And at that moment, the trap was sprung, but it wasn't for us. Kantakuzenos' men (what few were left to him) came up over the rise, fighting a running battle to hold back a band of Turkish cavalry, but came to the stream, which, though fordable, was too fast and too deep to fight through.

Some of us made to ford the stream from our side, but the Emperor ordered us back, fearing that this was exactly what the Turks wanted. While I knew in my head that the Emperor was right, this did not square with the reputation of Manuel Comnenus, who had often in the past been criticized for taking unwarranted risks, and had even been punished by his father John[59] (long before my time) for doing so.

Instead we moved forward, leaving our comrades to hold off the Turks as long as possible, hoping that another band of Romans would be close enough to come to their aid.

But none did.

And I feel compelled to mention at this point that no one besides the Emperor, myself included, had found anything wrong with the water, neither in taste nor colour.

But we marched alongside the Emperor, as I would by my oath still do this day, though an icy finger began to scratch at my heart, and an unwelcome voice began whispering in my ear that our leader's mind was becoming unhinged.

None of us could help looking over our shoulders at the desperate fight Kantakuzenos and his "little Greeks" put up against what we could now see were elite Turkish cavalry. Not a single Roman fell without accounting for at least one Turk, and at the last Kantakuzenos alone remained, encircled by the enemy, but refusing to surrender and be captured. He knew no help was coming, and he knew why, *understood* why. And yet my heart was shattering to pieces for the man who had without a second thought saved my life earlier in the day.

He rose high in his saddle like some champion of Greek myth, or better yet, some mead-hall saga, and saluted us in the distance.

I tried, in some vain hope that he would see it, to return the salute with my own raised sword, but he had already spurred his horse forward, a weapon in each hand and the reins in his teeth, cutting a bloody furrow through the enemy even as they dragged him down and cut him to pieces.

Thanks to that truly noble nobleman and those about him, we had put some distance between ourselves and the stream, but now the Turks forded it and were coming for us.

As I said, these were no ordinary Turks; their armour and weapons were chased with silver and gold, and the glint of gemstones could be seen on hilts and scabbards. And on their horses' trappings, too. Each and every steed was pure black and powerfully built, of the type they call Arabians, and had long, flowing manes with silver bells tied into them that tinkled as they rode.

Louder as they rode at us, faster and harder.

There were almost forty of them, and just slightly less of us. Some of us were mounted, but most were not. Some of us had shields, some set spears, but there was no question of a shield-wall. Yet at the same time, the Turks were not riding in any kind of formation; only each warrior spurring his own steed forward, he hoped, to glory.

And glory we would give them that day, or death. Whoever they were, we could not run from these Turks, we *would not* run. We were sick unto death of running.

Besides the Roman — or *Greek*, if you *must* — *kataphraktoi* with the Emperor, the rest of us who remained were Varangians, a mix of Englishmen like myself, Danes, Swedes, and still some Russians, as of old.

"Varyagi v pered!"[60] The old Russian command came loud and clear, I knew not from whom. It could have been the ghost of Basil the Bulgar-Slayer, for all I know, because I never did find out.

In a way, the command was ignored, for the *kataphraktoi* stepped up right next to us, as though the order had applied to them too. And so did the Emperor. And there was no time for anyone to protest or argue, for the first of those thundering black stallions were upon us.

There would be no tactical manoeuvres here, no strategy. It was just us against them, simple (and brutal) as that.

But our blood was also up; I know at least mine was. I had seen too many men (some just boys) felled by arrows from the heights, crushed by rocks. I had heard too many pleas for help that I couldn't answer. And I had just seen a "little Greek" who had saved *my* life go down fighting like a Viking berserker.

After all, were we not the inheritors of the traditions of those original Russians and Northmen whom Emperor Basil had imported to tip the scales in his civil war? It was almost as though a kind of energy flowed between us, man to man. And we had also inherited another tradition. That of the legions that had conquered the known world, destroyed the Persians at Nineveh, and kept the Picts to the north of Hadrian's Wall in Britain for centuries.

Yes, we were Greeks and Englishmen, Danes, Swedes, and Russians, all serving under the same banner. But we were also Vikings and *legionaries*, and we were going to fight and die as such.

I neither boast nor exaggerate, and I pray that you will believe me, sister, when I say that something went through me in those instants. I have been afraid many, many times on the battlefield, but in that one moment out of all the other times, I felt no fear. And no, it was not some berserk battle-fury out of the epic tales, but rather a kind of grim and absolute determination.

That we would prevail, and they would not. That *we* would live, and they would not.

A black stallion thundered past me on my left, but I paid it no attention, knowing that I was nowhere in range of the right-handed rider's gleaming scimitar. One or other of my brothers — my *real* brothers, dear sister — would deal with him. Only about two or three horse's-lengths behind came another Turk, lining me up for a scimitar-slash that, with the horse's momentum behind it, would have easily cut me in half.

As you will recall, I now carried no shield, and as the heathen thundered down on me, doubtless expecting to kill me and trample my remains without even stopping, I held my sword loosely in my only partially-functional left hand. I held that axe I had picked up in my right.

And again, I do not mean to boast, but only to thank God for all the days I spent practicing with that type of axe almost since I was strong enough to pick one up in one hand. You were there many of those hours growing up, and you've seen how I can throw.

Just as he brought his blade to the top of its intended arc, I threw. Probably the single most important throw of my life.

Direct hit.

Dead centre of the stallion's face. The blade bit through mail and into the horse's flesh beneath, but I guess not far enough to slice directly into its brain.

Nevertheless, as I sidestepped as the horse and rider plunged past, the stallion bucked and reared, screaming in terror and pain, my axe protruding from its forehead as though it were a chopping-block.

Having completely lost control, the Turk was thrown, hitting the ground hard. But I knew that right then, the out-of-control horse was a more immediate threat than its probably —

hopefully — wounded rider. Just as it passed me, I leaned in and chopped down hard with both hands now on my sword, and cleanly sheared off its right rear leg, below the reach of its barding.

I know you love horses, sister, and I promise you I took no joy in this. The horse was a weapon of the enemy, and as I said, it was them or us. Nor did I allow the beast's suffering to be prolonged. He was down, and I stepped round the back of him (to avoid the thrashing of his remaining legs), and, finding a seam where the components of his armour had separated, I swiftly decapitated him, and retrieved my axe from where he had shaken it loose.

I was now covered in new blood over all of the old that had dried already; it fountained from the stump of the stallion's neck.

Meanwhile, his master, who had lost his scimitar, was up on his hands and knees, and trying to crawl away. I just strode up behind him, and struck him back down to the ground, my axe biting deep into his back. Then, ignoring his gurgling protests or pleas, I put my knee into his back, and wrenched out the axe. Dropping my sword — which I still carried in my left hand for the moment — I seized him by the beard that overspilled his armour, and yanked his head back, cutting his throat wide open with the blade of my axe. Hands again bathed in still-pumping heart's-blood, I threw his face down into the dirt without even looking at it.

Grasping my sword-hilt in my left hand again, I rose, turning just in time to see another scimitar-armed Turk who had been rushing me on foot from behind, and was almost upon me, beginning to stab upwards at my face with the point of his blade.

I sidestepped just in time, striking at an angle with my axe to parry his blade and trap it with the beard[61], forcing it down. As I twisted to do that, I also brought up my sword, clubbing at his head with the flat of it. He managed to roll his head away from the blow, but only to go straight into the top of my axe-haft, which I had yanked loose from his scimitar to smash upwards into his teeth. He staggered backwards, and I moved with him, kicking one of his feet out before he could put his weight on it, and he landed flat down on his back, stunned for the only instant I needed. I had lost the axe when I struck him (probably because it was so slippery with blood), but I now put both hands on my sword in a reverse-grip, and drove down hard through armour, muscle, and bone, transfixing him to the filthy, blood-soaked earth.

Gulping air to give me strength, I stepped down on his chest to pull my blade back out through his convulsing body, and stepped clear, turning a quick circle in a defensive stance, waiting to see what would come at me next.

But it was over, for the moment.

The Romans had not won the day, but they had won the moment.

A half-dozen remaining Turks were fleeing for their lives, some two to a horse, others barely clinging to their mounts, while yet other beasts wandered riderless, going in whatever direction their confusion took them.

As for our side, at least half of us were still standing, including the Emperor, though he was bleeding from a gash on his right arm that another Varangian was attending to.

We bound one another's wounds, and quickly collected up gear and weapons, preparing to move on. I noticed that the scimitar of the first Turk I had slain had a good-sized jewel in its hilt. But the mood I was in, I didn't want to honour our enemies even by taking trophies, and I am — or was then — paid well enough. I ground it down with my bootheel into the bloody muck, in a kind of fury. This drew some glances, but no one said anything, each attending to his own duties.

The Turks we had defeated had clearly been important, high-ranking ones, so the Emperor (still maintaining presence of mind, as you see), ordered a thorough search of their persons and any captured saddlebags for anything that looked like a letter or a message, for an interpreter to look at later, if we still had any alive. I myself chose to stand watch rather than go through the dead men's things. Do not think that I don't understand the value of intelligence, I know it wins wars, but at that hour my only thought was that if another cursed heathen tried to come at us on this spot, *I* would be the first Roman he would have to go through.

And thus it was *my* eyes that were first to be blessed with the sight not of Turks, but of other bands of our comrades hastening over the crest to join us, a dozen here, another couple of dozen there.

And they brought news. They had heard the sounds of heavier fighting in the distance, farther to the rear. The way sound carried in those ravines, it could still have been a very considerable distance away, but it had seemed to have been moving closer. If true, it could only have meant that Kontostephanos' rearguard was fighting its way through whatever Turks remained in the ravine behind us.

This cheered each and every one of us, except, it seemed, the Emperor, who only gave the order to move out as soon as we were ready. This worried me at the time, and even more so saddened me when I later discovered its cause.

A significant number of us had gathered by that time, several score at least, so now we Varangians fell in around the Emperor, as was our normal duty, while the "little Greeks" now protected *our* flanks as we hastened forward. And protect us they did, from several attempts by different bands to ambush us, putting a bloodied enemy to flight every time.

For my own part, I participated in no more fighting that day, yet still managed to acquire another injury, seemingly from the spite of the very terrain itself. Stepping on what appeared to be solid gravel — it had even had a tiny shrub growing from it! — I suddenly fell through into a sinkhole of some sort almost five feet deep, twisting my back sharply in the process. I was quickly hauled out — although I would have been able to climb out on my own — and found that the muscles in my lower back (again on the left side!) had seized up painfully. It caused a significant limp, but before I could ask for a spear-shaft or something else to use as a crutch, Manuel himself ordered me onto a horse, brooking no protest from me. A *kataphraktus* graciously gave up his mount to me, and had to help me into the saddle. He then walked with us, leading his warhorse by the reins and whispering to it and patting it from time to time for so gently tolerating an unfamiliar rider.

This injury actually gave me more pain than any of my others, and yet again, this type of thing never seems to happen in the epic poems, does it?

No one knew what it had been for sure, a natural feature, or perhaps the remains of some ancient well. It was unlikely to have been a trap set by the enemy; it would probably have had sharpened stakes in it otherwise. In any event, we all stepped more cautiously moving forward.

As it was, I now rode close enough to the Emperor to see the shadow that had come over his face, and the way his eyes periodically flickered this way and that, not so much scanning for the enemy, as eyeing the men around him, particularly his fellow Greeks. He also looked back over his shoulder frequently. I made so bold as to address him directly, and ask if he was well, or if we could offer any assistance.

He only smiled, sadly, as though at some private thought, and thanked me with his customary grace, shaking his head no. And then he said something that both warmed and chilled my heart at the same time, a great compliment, but very strange. "I trust *you*, Eadric," calling me by name, yet putting his emphasis on the word *you*, as though there were others around us whom he could not. This troubled me greatly, as I believe it did the handful of others close enough to hear it.

We had gone another couple, or maybe three miles in this manner, our "little Greek" escort continuing to beat off attacks by Turkman warbands of varying sizes, when a shout went up that a large force had been sighted directly in front of us. Before we even had time to be dismayed, they were recognized as troops of our own *tagmas*, with Constantine Makrodoukas at the head of them.

We all gave breath to prayers of thanksgiving and sighs of at least temporary relief, as this meant that the vanguard and the *tagmatic* troops really had, at the beginning of the battle, been able to break through as we had been told, before we had lost all communication.

As we gratefully merged into their ranks, we found out that they had indeed seized a hill and managed, despite being under constant attack, to build a fortified marching camp, to which they would now escort us. The Turks were doing their best to invest the camp, but Makrodoukas and his fellow senior officers had been becoming very concerned at the delay in the arrival of any more of our troops. Consequently, he had detached and led a considerable force to go back along the trail in search of us.

A hearty cheer went up as we entered the gate, and though the Emperor acknowledged it (as did the rest of us), the shadow did not leave his face. He did not make a circuit of the camp to greet and inspect his men, as was his usual wont, but we rather made straight for the makeshift Imperial tent (the actual one having been lost with the baggage-train) that had been set up for him. I imagine many of the soldiers thought that he was hurrying to take council with his senior officers, but I knew he needed to just rest (as did we all), at least for a short time, and await news of the rearguard.

The Angelos brothers and their comrades had done a superb job, considering the conditions. They had not only been able to push through the Turks and seize this hill, but construct a well-fortified marching-camp while fending off constant attacks. Equipped only with the entrenching-tools they had had with them, and the gnarled trees and saplings in the immediate area, they had thrown up earthen walls fronted by ditches filled with sharpened stakes, enclosing enough room to accommodate the greater part of our original force (in rather cramped quarters, of course, but that would have had to be expected), and a natural spring, which would provide us with enough water if we managed it carefully. The scope of their accomplishment was made all the more clear by the fact that you could not have gone ten paces on that approach without encountering a corpse belonging to one side or the other.

Even this, though, would be only a brief respite, as there was no fodder for the remaining horses, and also precious little for the remaining men. In any protracted siege, we would have had to slaughter the mounts for food, and then we would *all* have been infantry.

Since my duty was to be in the Emperor's presence, I didn't have to do any perimeter patrols nor perform any other guard duties. My condition at this point wouldn't have made for much walking anyway.

Although I was granted dispensation (due to my injury) to sit (on a rock or the ground) in the Emperor's presence inside the Imperial tent, my nerves kept me going in and out, often settling myself on a crude bench just outside the tent's entrance.

A physician who had been attached to the *tagmata* attended to me, cleaning and bandaging or re-bandaging my wounds, and assuring me that nothing in my hand had been broken; it was just swelling. He massaged my lower back for a few minutes, rubbing something into it that seemed to loosen it a little. He told me he would have liked to put a poultice on it, but he was very short of supplies. I assured him I understood, and that there were men injured far worse than myself. He also told me that he believed, even after cleaning it, that the wound on my neck might be infected, but that he would look at it again tomorrow before cutting.

If any of us had a tomorrow.

Expecting to have to fight again the next day, if not sooner, I sought assistance from a comrade who was by no means a professional armourer, but had acquired a well-deserved reputation for temporary field-fixes. He provided me with a small round shield, no more than eighteen inches across, but with a heavy metal boss in its centre that could be used effectively as a clubbing weapon. He rigged the straps to be clasped so tightly over my wrist that I was unlikely to have it knocked away, and would be able to control it somewhat with the lower three (working) fingers of my hand. The lighter weight of this "target" shield would also be easier on my back.

I exchanged my regular blade for a shorter stabbing sword (like the old Roman *gladius*), as I expected to be fighting at close quarters. (Someone had suggested that I try to act as an archer, if my left hand could stand up to the pressure of drawing a bow. I had declined, as I have never been very good at archery, even at hunting. And in any case, a dark cast of mind had befallen me too, and I was determined to kill or die face-to-face.)

My friend also cleverly affixed two heavy four-inch iron nails to the metal on the top of my right-hand gauntlet, which I still wore, extending from the first and third knuckles if I made a fist to punch. Just about the right distance apart for a man's pair of eyes.

I need not remind you, sister, that this was no children's game.

Lastly, I rounded up another pair of "bearded" axes (slightly damaged) to put in my belt. Probably my favourite, most trusted weapon, if someone forced me to choose only one.

Small bands of battered survivors kept coming through the gates from time to time, but the shadows of dusk were already casting their pall over us when word came that the long-awaited rearguard had been sighted. As they passed into the camp it was obvious that while they too had been bloodied and definitely been in a fight, they had come through much more intact than any of the other divisions.

The Angelos brothers and the *tagmatic* commanders came out to greet Kontostephanos and his men, but the Emperor did not, and I knew in the pit of my stomach that this boded ill.

By the time the last of them were in, full darkness had fallen, as quickly as it always does in mountainous regions. We knew not in precisely what way, but every man was certain in his heart that the coming night would severely test the mettle and resolve of every last one of us.

I went into the Imperial tent, hoping to hear for myself what had taken place behind us.

I was taken aback, and honestly shaken by the reception Kontostephanos received.

Manuel questioned him harshly, in a manner bordering on the insulting, demanding what had taken him so long to follow and support his (our) division. Casting aside any traditional notions of Imperial reserve, Manuel paced up and down, relating the hardships the rest of us had been through, the heroic deaths of Baldwin and Kantakuzenos, stopping just short of accusing the dumbfounded Kontostephanos of cowardice or treason or maybe both. But he might as well not have stopped short, for he ended by kicking over a trestle and swearing "by all that is in Heaven and Hell and everywhere between" that *he*, Manuel, would not be another Diogenes.[62]

That was tantamount to an accusation of treason if there ever was one. Over a century ago, the Emperor Romanus Diogenes, who had been a fine soldier and general, had also led a large army into far eastern Anatolia, where he met the Seljuks near the shores of Lake Van. But Romanus' army wasn't defeated, it disintegrated on the field, due to the plotting of several of his chief nobles, particularly of the Ducas family. Not only that, but Romanus himself was personally betrayed to the Turks, who viciously blinded him and paraded him around in a cage like a captured beast. And then even more cruelly gifted (or sold) him to a rebel pretender to the Imperial throne who used him as a figurehead for his own treason.

It is a great credit to Kontostephanos that he remained calm in the face of what everyone present knew was an unwarranted attack. And everyone also knew that there was something very wrong, that this was not the Manuel Comnenus that many of us had known for years. Those looks he had been casting about him earlier quickly came back to mind. And for me, the remark, honour that it had been and was, that he trusted *me*. Who was it then that he *didn't* trust, and why?

Kontostephanos asked leave to explain his actions, and the Emperor had not gone so far down whatever mad road he had set himself upon that he did not grant it.

The rearguard, the veteran general explained, had remained at the entrance to the pass on the western side, to ensure that the Turks did not enter it *behind* the Emperor's division, and so be able to hem us in on four sides, rather than just three, as his orders had been. Once the Emperor's division had fully deployed into the pass, he had allowed time for them to make sufficient progress, which his (Kontostephanos') scouts had reported they were doing. He had then sent other scouting parties in force to make sure the heights on either side of his route stayed clear. Yes, he took his time, but he was doing what he should have. (You must also keep in mind that although we knew we might face one, we did not *want* to fight a battle in the pass, we just wanted to get through it.)

Consequently, the rearguard did not commit to fully entering the pass until probably *after* disaster had struck Baldwin's right wing and the baggage-train. They proceeded with caution, which is the whole point of a rearguard; it is often used similarly to a reserve, being saved as long as possible, in order to be deployed to the point of greatest need, not just anywhere that there happens to be fighting. So even if they were aware of the sounds of the clash of arms from up the pass ahead of them, they were still to proceed with caution, so as to be able to perform their task the most effectively. (This is not the same thing as simply proceeding off the field and going home, which is what the accursed Ducas did a century ago at Manzikert.)

By the time they reached the wreckage of the baggage-train, *we* had already fought our way past it, and the Turkmen (whose greed trumps their discipline, as I said) were busy pillaging it.

Kontostephanos and his men fell upon the looters in force, and were able to kill a considerable number of them before putting the rest to flight. Although many of those who escaped did so with pilfered coin and items of monetary value, Kontostephanos did not make the mistake of pursuing them into the hills where the Turkmen would have had the advantage.

The route we had cleared had been of considerable assistance to him, but rather than moving on right away, he undertook a task that we had been unable to. With axe and hammer, he and his men set about destroying as much of the still-intact siege-equipment as they could without fire, in order that it not fall into enemy hands to be used against us at some later date.

He took the time to do this, aside from the very good reason just stated, because even though he could see that we had suffered severe losses, some of us at least had fought through, and if the enemy was still pursuing us, it could actually have been to our advantage to lull them into believing that no one was pursuing *them*.

They had then advanced somewhat more quickly over the same ground we had, and Kontostephanos confessed that, upon seeing the carnage there at that time, he believed he might have been fatally mistaken in not making more haste. (Most of us, myself included, did not think that he had, and rather that his ability to keep his division largely intact had given us one of our best hopes of still getting out of this alive.) But the bands of Turks they had encountered after that were easily bested, usually just fleeing before the obvious strength of his force, and he soon began to overtake straggling Romans who had been part of ours.

His calm explanation and the directness and humility with which he delivered it seemed to mollify the Emperor for the time being, probably because virtually every other officer appeared to accept that his actions had been reasonable and prudent.

And yet Manuel still seemed to be unable to sit or stand in one place for long, getting up and down and pacing continually, as well as shooting strange, searching looks at this man or that, when he thought they didn't notice.

Knowing he had other Varangians in the tent to guard him, and knowing also in my heart of hearts that no one in there meant him any harm, I returned to my seat outside the entrance.

It was one of those nights when the watchfires seem less to light the dark, than to simply push it back a little, beyond which point it seemed even blacker than it normally had any right to be. There was very little moonlight, diffused as it was by clouds, or possibly even some remains of the dust-storm we had battled through earlier.

And as the darkness pressed in around us, so, it seemed, did the Turkmen, shouting their war cries and worse. There were many among the Roman troops who were of mixed blood. Due to the upheavals and territorial losses following Diogenes' ill-fated campaign, this emperor's (Manuel's) father and grandfather had spent much of the intervening century reclaiming significant parts of that territory (although the far east of Anatolia remained lost), and Manuel had been building on that; this very campaign had been meant as a capstone to those efforts.

Thus many troops came from regions that had suffered Turkish occupation — even though they had been back in Roman hands for two generations — and thereby had a working knowledge of at least the Turkish spoken language.

Those circling the camp came close enough to be heard, without being targeted by any archers we still had for sentry duty. Threats and promises almost as disruptive as spears or arrows were hurled into our camp throughout the night. Threats that on the morrow we would all share the fate of Vatatzes, and of our brothers, whose bodies filled the ditches the length of the ravine. Promises, that if their "kinsmen" deserted the Emperor and went over to the Sultan, they would not only be spared, but richly rewarded. (After converting, or in some cases maybe converting back, to Islam, of course.)

To the best of my knowledge, no one took them up on their

offers.

There was to be little or no sleep in our camp that night. I was glad to see that there was the usual sharpening of weapons and inspection of equipment, without anyone having had to be ordered to carry these things out; despite their fear, or perhaps because of it, the men were still readying themselves to fight. There were, as to be expected, many prayers. But I also noted that some, even more than usual, sought out their kinsmen, or clan relations, even outside of their own fighting units, in order to sit and talk quietly in their small groups before the flickering watchfires, when they were not on perimeter patrol.

I believe that they feared that they were seeing their blood relatives for the last time on this earth by that firelight, and although I believe they were prepared to fight on the morrow to their last drops of blood, I am also certain that most of them never expected to see the next sunset. Or their wives. Or their children, or their parents.

I had already made my weapons as ready as they would ever be, and thought, despite the situation, to try to get some rest. There were other men standing guard at the Imperial tent's entrance, so I moved off to the side a little, finding a horse-blanket to spread on the ground. And so I laid myself down to rest, but, as they say, with one eye open.

But whatever malaise had affected the ranks crept its way also into the Imperial tent, where its vine blossomed into sick, poisonous fruit.

I had been lying down for I am sure no more than half an hour, drifting in that border-realm between waking and sleep, the one in which we are often stalked by the worst things our imaginations can conjure. I was snapped back to full wakefulness by the sound of a clatter and partially-raised voices.

I was up immediately, despite my pain, hand on the hilt of my borrowed *gladius*. The doorguards had already stepped into the tent, and one of them whispered to me as I came through, "It's the

Emperor, he's gone mad! He wants to flee right now!"

If I was some type of poet, I would tell you how the torchlight and shadows danced across the faces in that tent, illuminating fear and anger, but even more, shock and dismay. Everyone was on their feet, Kontostephanos was an arm's-length from the Emperor, grasping Manuel's shoulders, and the Emperor appeared to be trying to tear free of his grip, as though to stalk past him. Constantine Angelos also had a hand on the Emperor's forearm. Kontostephanos was urging the Emperor to stop and think, but the Emperor was shaking his head, and the light glinted off a wildness in his eyes that I had never seen before.

The others in the tent were advancing on the three of them, and I was terrified of what might happen if they got there.

My heart in my throat, I roared, "Varangians, stand fast! Weapons stay in sheaths, damn it!" I had no technical rank above the other guards, but neither did any of them over me. I suppose it was a manifestation of those "leadership qualities" the *hetaireiarch* (who himself lay somewhere amongst the mountains of bodies several miles back) had kept telling me I possess.

The scene was frozen for a moment, and longer than it should have been, because I had really walked myself into a bear pit, and had to think very quickly.

"Your Majesty, *Basileus*," I addressed the Emperor directly, "you only hours ago said that you trusted me. Have I done anything since that time to stop deserving that trust?"

He looked at me for a second, and then shook his head, but there was an air of confusion to it.

Nevertheless, I went on: "Then I beg of you, Your Majesty, in the name of Christ and all His saints, trust me *now*."

I bowed slightly to Angelos and Kontostephanos, without taking my eyes off them. "My Lords," I said. "I beg of you to remove your hands from the Emperor's person. And I beg your pardons, but keep them away from your weapons." They nodded and complied. To their credit (and my relief), they did so without any hesitation or body language meant to convey their superiority over me.

"Your Majesty," I continued with just a little less tension, "You know that I will carry out any order of yours, and follow you anywhere, though it mean my certain death. But I know these men, and I know they mean you no harm. Neither I nor my brothers would allow any harm to come to you. I beg of you that you hear their counsels, weigh them, but of course, your decision will be our command."

Both Angelos and Kontostephanos nodded solemnly, and finally the Emperor did, too, appearing to regain some of his composure. My own heart only then began to slow, and I began to breathe again, still not quite able to believe what I had just done — what I had just dared do.

Someone hurried to right the stool and trestle the Emperor had knocked over. Manuel sunk down onto the stool, sighing.

"I thank you all," he rasped, " and *Basileus* or no *Basileus*, I apologize for my conduct." He smiled ruefully as he touched fingers to his bandaged head, and told us that he had not been feeling himself, but that it was no excuse, as so many others had suffered much greater injuries in his name. He then asked that we all step out and get some rest, he would confer with his officers alone.

Reluctantly, we complied with his request.

Once outside, I heard what had taken place before I had come in. The Emperor, having allowed his head injury's dressing to be changed, and his other injuries tended to, had sat in silence for some time. He had still refused to take any water, no matter how many assurances he was given that it was drawn from an unpolluted spring. So instead a little wine was found for him, which I'm not sure helped matters.

He had appeared as though only partially listening to his officers, while his thoughts also wandered in some faraway places all his own.

Then (as I heard it), he suddenly rose from his stool, knocking it over, and looking wildly around the room, threw over the trestle and strode towards the entrance. He snarled (my source's word, not mine) that he would take only his most trusted bodyguards and slip out of camp under cover of darkness, killing anyone who tried to stop him, again comparing himself to Romanus Diogenes, caught in a nest of vipers. He also said that *his* head would not be displayed on a pike's end, like that of Vatatzes.

It had been then that Angelos and Kontostephanos had tried to restrain him, saying that he had no traitors about him; he needed only recall how many noble men had fallen fighting when the odds were against them. He was in the midst of his own loyal army, which, battered and bloodied as it was, was still sizeable, and still could and would fight for him. Would he abandon them now to death or capture by the Turks? What heart would they have to fight if their leader abandoned them? They were *his* men, his responsibility. And what of those who awaited them in their homes, in sleepless dread? He had tried to break free of them, and others were about to intervene, and you know the rest.

What was discussed in the Imperial tent after that, I know not, other than that Manuel abandoned any idea of flight. None of the courses that were available to us were very palatable, but, as the generals had emphasized to Manuel, we still had an intact army and a defensible position. And although we had probably lost more than one man in every four, we still had a sizeable force, including walking wounded.

But what strategies were debated or decided I cannot tell you, because I spent the rest of the night outside, as much by my own choice as by obedience to orders. I loved the Emperor as though he were my own blood, and it filled me with dread to see the condition he was in. He seemed to have shaken it off (at least for now) with the help of men that he should surely have never doubted he could trust with his life, but what if that fey mood suddenly took him again?

I was uneasy, no, almost sick with fear, and not this time of the enemy, but of the state of mind of my own leader. Nevertheless, I knew that in the end I would follow whatever orders he gave me, no matter how ignominious, or how suicidal (which I probably would have preferred).

Thus passed the night, and just as dawn broke, a large contingent of Turks attacked the camp, in an attempt to draw the noose tighter. They shot hundreds of arrows over the earthworks, killing and wounding a number of men who were nearest the outer perimeter. Fortunately for us, though, the soldiers of the vanguard who had entrenched the camp had provided enough cover positions to prevent this kind of attack from becoming a massacre.

Unfortunately, we no longer had enough archers to respond effectively. (Many men tried to swell their numbers, but there is quite a difference between a man who has drawn a bow once or twice and a professional archer.)

Consequently, the Emperor (having at least for the time being recovered his resolve), ordered a sortie to drive them back, and a contingent of the original vanguard troops (heavy infantry) was sent out under John Angelos, but had only middling success. They (wisely) retreated back into the camp before the swift Turkish horsemen drew them out far enough to encircle them (which had, of course, been their plan).

Another attempt immediately followed, this time involving the cavalry elements of the eastern *tagmata*, commanded by Constantine Makrodoukas, who was able to come to grips more closely with the enemy, and bloody them some as they retreated, but again, our forces withdrew without giving chase; the Turks were just trying to set the same trap again. And finding that it wasn't going to work.

Perhaps — *probably* — it was for this reason that the Turkish forces withdrew and ceased their attacks, and it was very shortly afterwards that word came from our lookouts that an embassy under a flag of truce was approaching. They were requesting entry to our camp, and an audience with the Emperor to propose terms of peace. (Surely they were not contemplating that we would surrender; our actions of that very morning should have made that very clear.)

Now there are those who say that this was some type of miracle, and that it happened solely because God moved the Sultan's heart to mercy towards the Christians, convincing him to allow them to go unharmed, rather than slaughtering them, as he was in a position to. That somehow, the Romans had been being punished for *hubris* (a special Greek word for a surfeit of pride), but that now, Our Lord saw the punishment to have been sufficient. And they support these views with all sorts of references to Scripture.

Again, I pray that I utter no blasphemy against the very One who has preserved me through so many battles, including this one, but this is utter nonsense.

To begin with, we had taken the field against the enemies of Christendom, and a serious threat thereto. And our force included not only Romans and their allies, but also Crusaders from Jerusalem and Antioch. And although I pray that God grant each and every one of their noble souls eternal peace, I have to say that we came out a great deal better than the Templars did the following year in their encounter with Saladin.

In my opinion — and it is an informed one — those tend to be the views of persons whom I believe to be the Emperor's true political enemies. And as God and Christ are my witnesses, not one of them had been within four hundred miles of the battle.

Maybe we were being punished for *something* — how can I really know? But I do know that it was God's grace and mercy that strengthened our arms, allowing us to fight our way out of a desperate situation. While I know that I cannot pretend to have knowledge of the ways of Our Lord, all the evidence of my eyes points to His having bolstered our hearts, not having weakened that of the Sultan.

As I said already, we were battered and bloodied, but far from destroyed. The prospect of taking Iconium had of course been lost with the baggage-train, but we still accounted for a fighting force to be reckoned with — especially if the Sultan tried to completely reduce or destroy us, as he would have been up against desperate men fighting for their lives with nothing to lose. The cost in casualties to him would have been enormous. And he might not even have been certain of victory then.

How so, you no doubt ask, dear sister, if he had us surrounded? As I told you before, Kilidj Arslan is heavily dependent upon the half-wild Turkmen who ride under his banner in return for the promise of spoils. By this point, many of those had doubtless already ridden off, having gotten what they came for when they despoiled the baggage-train of considerable wealth. Many of the others probably saw that there was little more plunder to be had — at least not without a desperate fight — and as a result, the Sultan was probably bleeding manpower by the hour, and soon would have only his regular army — which make no mistake, was formidable — to reduce us with.

If we managed to break out, the damage to the Turkish-held countryside would be nightmarish. Either we would ravage it ourselves for supplies, burning crops and taking prisoners, or the Turks would have had to evacuate their civilians as best they could, and burn their own crops and stores to deny them to us. None of that would have appealed to the Sultan's nobles, and especially not those whose estates and landholdings would be directly affected.

So instead the Sultan sent an embassy headed by a renegade Greek named Gabras.

Manuel granted safe passage, but his armed escort was detained just inside the gate, while Gabras and his aides were allowed to proceed under heavy guard (as no one believed the Turks to be above sending a suicide-assassin).

They were received by the Emperor in front of what passed for the Imperial tent, with Manuel sitting on a large trestle that had been covered with clean cloth and set up as a makeshift throne, with the Imperial banner flying right above it. The Emperor was surrounded by his surviving senior officers, and *us*, his Varangian Guard.

This creature Gabras, whom I took an instantaneous and extreme dislike to, made a great show of obeisance to the Emperor, his nose nearly scraping the ground as he bowed, giving greetings from his sovereign to the very one who should properly have been called that, by all that is right and godly. He then proceeded to enumerate the gifts that he had brought from his master, all the while reminding Manuel of the "years of friendship" that had persisted between the two rulers.

Gabras had brought with him a magnificent horse outfitted with silver trappings that had come from one of the Sultan's special stables, which housed only animals used in solemn processions marking important occasions. He also presented Manuel with a finely crafted two-handed, double-edged sword (hilt-first, and *slowly*, of course, or he would have died right there).

Despite the (very real) threat of an assassination attempt, Manuel had overruled his officers (and his guards) in his decision to not have the persons of Gabras and his aides searched before coming into close proximity with him. He had said something about it presenting a confident air to the enemy, but that made no sense to me, and I (as well as others probably) marked it up to the injury that kept him from being quite himself.

So we were watching Gabras' people closely, our own hands near, but not quite resting on our weapons. At first, I had posted myself just off the Emperor's left hand, but after Gabras had presented his gifts, and asked permission to approach the Emperor more intimately, in order that he could speak more quietly and privately, I signaled another Varangian to take my place, which he immediately did. Myself, I advanced several paces to stand very close to a particularly shifty-looking Turk, whose eyes I didn't like at all. I had looked over Gabras' companions as best I could, and thought that if there *was* an assassin, it was that one. (It surely wouldn't have been Gabras himself, men like him value their own skins too much for that type of work.)

So despite my own discomfort, I stood as close to my man as I could without actually touching him, and I knew my attempt to make *him* uncomfortable (and throw him off any plan he might have had) was successful. I made sure he saw me casually flex my gauntleted fist with the two spikes on it, and gave him a little smile when I did so. Just a little one.

In any event, perhaps my suspicions were unfounded, because no violence erupted.

But as a result, I missed most of what passed between the Emperor and Gabras. Manuel had affected a chilly manner at first, but had then, by all accounts, appeared to thaw somewhat as various remarks passed between them. Finally, Gabras spoke a little louder, as though he meant for others to hear, some ridiculous comment about the yellowish dust, and how it had discoloured the Emperor's surcoat (which he wore over his mail), and how he was saddened to see such an unlucky hue (in time of war) upon the person of so noble a ruler as Manuel.

At this, Manuel smiled, and, standing up, removed the Imperial garment, with its purple and gold embroidery, and gifted it to that dog on the spot.

I suppose that was the right thing to do, because within minutes, peace terms were agreed. Manuel accepted the Sultan's gifts, and documents were drawn up to which Manuel and Gabras (representing Kilidj Arslan, who no doubt had received no injuries, nor collected any dust of any colour on his person) set their hands. The Roman army was to be allowed safe passage back to Imperial territory, but the Emperor was required to demolish the newly-repaired fortifications of Dorylaeum and Sublaeum.

Pursuant to the treaty, the main part of the Turkish army withdrew, leaving only small escort parties to see us back across our borders. As we dismantled our camp and gathered our gear, thousands of prayers of thanksgiving went up for Our Lord's deliverance of us from the very jaws of the Archenemy.

Little did we know that we had not yet been served out our last measures of horror for the day.

Although the Emperor had requested that we be escorted out of Seljuk territory by some different, more wholesome route, we were denied this, the Sultan once again showing his true colours.

We were forced to march (or ride, like me) right back through every mile, every single pace the of hell that we had fought through the previous day. The bodies of the dead lay piled in every direction, limbs entangled, some filling ditches and shallow ravines to overflowing. The stench overwhelmed us, and many of us were overcome by merciless vomiting, until we had not even saliva left to spit. As we approached, clouds of carrion birds lifted into the air to blot out the uncaring sky, filling our ears with their angry cries at our interruption of their feasting.

Some of the dead were no doubt the very men who had pleaded with us just yesterday for help, only to see us pass them by as though we cared not at all, though it cut us to the very quick.

Many cried out as they thought they recognized their kinsmen or close comrades among the bodies. Myself, I kept my eyes straight forward as much as I could, knowing I could do nothing for any of the fallen. But what I couldn't avoid seeing, especially being higher up because I was riding, sickened me even further.

The Turks, while we were sheltering in our camp, had not only stripped the bodies, but had desecrated them in a terrible, bestial manner. First, in many cases, the Turks had taken scalps, as is the custom among some of their wilder clans. But that was not the worst.

Most of the corpses had had their private parts cut off. The likely reason for this was that even though we were not going to be given the opportunity to recover our dead in any event, we could not tell the circumcised from the uncircumcised[63] amongst the bodies. Our suspicion was that they did this to hide the fact that we had killed a larger number of them than we had thought or they were willing to admit.

If they had any other reason, it doesn't bear thinking about.

And maybe even worst of all, there were scrawny, sickly-looking figures, dressed in rags and scraps of skins, crawling among the dead, looking for any item of least value that the Turks had left behind. It was hard to even tell if they were men or women, so emaciated and filthy they were, but some were so small that they could only have been children. Their appearances — and movements — were more animal than human. I don't know if they lived somewhere hidden amongst this forbidding terrain, hiding from civilization of any kind, probably still praying to animals and rocks (or worse things), or if they came from somewhere else, following the Turks. Or maybe the corpses themselves just bred these scavengers like maggots, as they seem to on every battlefield, no matter its location. I hoped, as I always do when I see such wretches, that their greed and desecration of the noble dead (of both sides) is rewarded by some painful rotting disease that sends them swiftly back to whatever hell spawned them.

When we had finally come to the end of this charnel passage, our escorts turned and left us to return to their compatriots, just as we neared the western end of the pass.

Almost immediately, and before we could get completely out of the pass, we were assailed by bands of mounted Turkmen from the rear. Many feared that Arslan had reneged on his undertakings, and had ordered his men to try to finish the task they had so eagerly begun.

However, this was not the case; it was just another example of how precarious the Sultan's control over the tribesmen was. They were able to pick off a few unfortunates who had survived all of the foregoing only to die of an arrow in the back, almost, as a poet might say, in sight of hearth and home. But our rearguard put those bands to flight with little difficulty, and indeed, their dead were probably more numerous than ours.

But the fact that these attacks were somehow permitted to take place at all outraged the Emperor, and he considered it a breach of Arslan's undertaking. Thus, on the return journey, replying as he said in kind, we dismantled Sublaeum, but not Dorylaeum (which was by far the more important of the two).

Retracing our earlier route, we finally reached Chonai, where most of the army remained to recuperate, Manuel making special provisions for the care of the sick and wounded. Then Manuel and those of us in his guard went on to Philadelphia, where he took (and gave us) several days to rest before returning to Constantinople.

It was from there that Manuel sent missives ahead describing the outcome of the expedition, and although they all originated from him, they did not all seem to agree with one another, or even form a coherent whole. In the more public ones, the Sultan had had no choice but to sue for peace once the Roman army had forced the pass. But in more private messages, he (again comparing himself to Diogenes) lamented this terrible blow to the Imperial re-conquest of Anatolia, and the even more terrible loss of lives and treasure. These were no mere words; as I have told you, Manuel cared for his soldiers deeply. Many of us had come to feel like his adopted sons, and all were proud to serve him. Which makes the events that night in that tent all the more inexplicable.

For my own part, I know it was a defeat, because it would be a long time before a force that powerful could be put together again, equipped for such a single, determined purpose. And yet our army had not been trapped and destroyed as the Sultan had no doubt hoped that it would. The better part of our army, despite our grievous losses, came back out bloodied, but intact. And if anyone survived who had marched out as a green recruit, he was a battle-hardened veteran now. And as for the Turks, we all believed, and I still do believe, from what I saw, that their losses were far greater than they would ever admit.

And here it is time for me to—*finally*—draw this account to a close. You already know the rest, about how Arslan sent a punitive attack the next year in response to Manuel's refusal to dismantle Dorylaeum, and how it was defeated. And how our expeditions that next year, with the Emperor participating personally in some, met with success, including the one I fought in at Panasium.

I have written far more, and in more detail than I had ever intended, and slept little.

Know then, dear sister, that you and Henry are forever in my heart, the sun and the moon to me. And though I hope and pray that someday we will all see each other again, please know this, and remember me, and see that Henry does too:

I was a member of the Varangian Guard in Constantinople, where I served in the army of the one true Roman Emperor. I fought for Manuel Comnenus.

Forever your loving brother and uncle,

Eadric

AFTERWORD:

While I have of course elaborated on the primary historical sources in some places for dramatic effect, I have tried to follow them as closely as possible.

Many historians actually consider Myriocephalon to have been a greater disaster than Manzikert, largely because the energetic Comnenian emperors were at least able to stabilize the situation and recover some significant territory after Alexius I (r. 1081 – 1118) seized the throne. Yet, as was indicated in the "Translator's Note", despite some successes in the following years, Myriocephalon seemed to have broken Manuel I (r. 1143 – 80) in some way that pushed the Empire's fortunes into a spiral that went from bad to worse to outright disaster.

Much has been written in the secondary literature, usually centring on how not only the destruction of his grand design to conquer Iconium once and for all, but that, coupled with his "dark night of the soul" during which he — *extremely uncharacteristically* — considered flight, completely changed the Emperor, leaving him a haunted man who was never the same again.

I have not the expertise to do so, but I am respectfully suggesting that Manuel's behaviour, as recorded in the sources that this tale is based upon, be examined in the light of what we in the third decade of the twenty-first century now know about two things, the first of which is post-traumatic stress disorder. This has, I believe, been suggested before.

But I do not believe that the following has. Virtually every account of the battle mentions the episode of Manuel being found alone and dismounted, resting under the shade of a wild pear tree. *With his helmet having been knocked askew and him being unable to fix it on his own*, until he received assistance.

What had happened? The one thing that is virtually certain is that Manuel took a blow to the head at some point. But what kind of blow? A mace? A rock? Or did he fall from his horse and hit his head? The sources tell us nothing, because apparently no one actually saw (or survived to tell) what happened to him, presumably because of the blinding dust-storm. But neither does Manuel tell anyone (as far as we know) anything.

Now I know it is usually considered *verboten* for historians to argue from silence, but here I feel compelled to. As I had Eadric point out in our tale, Manuel was not wearing intricate plate that would have required the attention of an armourer. So why couldn't he fix his own helmet? Was he still dazed (perhaps following a blackout, which might explain him not remembering how he got hit)? Was he having difficulties with his coordination?

Like PTSD, we now, thanks not only to the military, but also professional sports leagues like the NHL, the NFL, the CFL, FIFA, and others, not to mention growing interest in the medical community generally, know a great deal more about concussion and traumatic brain injuries than we did even twenty years ago.

As I said, I have no expertise in the area, but I suggest that it may be an interesting and fruitful line of inquiry for someone who does to more closely examine, in that light, Manuel's subsequent actions not only at Myriocephalon, but over the last four years of his life following the battle.

Stephen S. Bondar

May, 2021

Maxwell, Christchurch

Barbados, West Indies

[1]Niketas Choniates, *O City of Byzantium, Annals of Niketas Choniates.* ed. and trans. Harry J. Margoulias (Detroit: Wayne State Univ. Press, 1984).
[2] A.A. Vasiliev, "Manuel Comnenus and Henry Plantagenet", in *Byzantinische Zeitschrift* 29 (1929-30), pp. 233-44.
[3] Choniates, *op. cit.*
[4] John Haldon, *Warfare, State, and Society in the Byzantine World. (London: Routledge, 2003).*
[5] For those interested in a detailed analysis of Manuel Comnenus' reign, *cf.* Paul Magdalino, *The Empire of Manuel I Komnenos:1143-1180 (Cambridge Univ. Press,2003).* For the "Prester John" letter , *cf.* Robert Silverberg, *The Realm of Prester John* (New York: Doubleday, 1972).
[6] *Murrain* – A type of cattle disease.
[7] *To "take the Cross"* — refers to the oath taken by those going on Crusade, and in the common usage of the time, was often used as an expression for the undertaking itself.
[8] *"Cain to his Pharaoh"* — Here, of course, Eadric is referring to the Old Testament books of Genesis and Exodus. He refuses to commit fratricide as Cain did when he murdered Abel, and although the comparison is inexact, he likens his own brother to the Egyptian pharaoh who, ignoring Moses' repeated petitions (and threats), continued to "harden his heart" and refuse to release the Israelites from bondage.
[9] The term "Byzantine" was coined by German historians long after the Empire's demise in 1453, and was derived from the ancient name of its capital, Byzantium, a rather minor city until Constantine I (r.305 – 37), re-founded it as Constantinople, the capital of not only the Roman Empire in the East, but the Empire as a whole. While the western provinces fell away one by one, culminating in the Vandal capture of Rome in 456 and the deposition of Romulus Augustulus, the last western emperor, the eastern provinces survived the cataclysms of the fifth century. Although after about two hundred years, the Empire became, not only in terms of administration, but also in culture, predominantly (if not overwhelmingly) Greek in character, its citizens to the very last day considered themselves Romans, and their emperors to be the direct heirs of Augustus Caesar.
[10] Nicephorus II Phocas (r.963-69).
[11] *Saracen* – Here Eadric is using one of the alternative terms employed by the Byzantines in relation to the Muslims. Also common were *Hagarenes* and *Ishmaelites*, both referring to the tradition of the first Muslims, the peoples of the Arabian Peninsula, being descended from Ishmael, the Hebrew patriarch Abraham's illegitimate first son by his wife Sarah's maid Hagar, prior to (the previously thought to be barren) Sarah's conception of Isaac.
[12] The reader will remark here that, even if there had been any doubt before as to where Eadric's heart truly lies, it is certainly dispelled as he begins, without qualification, to resort to "we" and "our".
[13] *"Purple-born"*-Purple was *the* Imperial colour, and wearing garments of that colour was restricted by law (with severe penalties thereunder) to the Imperial family, and a very privileged and select few others. Whenever possible, empresses and princesses of the Immediate Imperial family delivered in a special birthing chamber whose walls were hung entirely with purple cloth and tapestries. The long association of purple with nobility goes back as far as the ancient Phoenicians, who first extracted purple dye from the shell of a particular mollusk; hence its rarity and value.
[14] *"Some book generations ago"* — Here Eadric is no doubt alluding to the *Book of Ceremonies* attributed to Constantine VII (r.944 – 59) [ed. Niebuhr, Bonn:1829].

[15] The student of this period of history will recognize how chillingly accurate this prediction (as well as some others) of Eadric's turned out to be.
[16] The closest English approximation of the second prince's name is Dhū'-n-Nun, so perhaps Eadric can be forgiven this lapse!
[17] This is no small thing that Eadric speaks of. Many rulers throughout history have maintained foreign bodyguards, specifically (among other reasons) *because* they couldn't understand what was said in their presence.
[18] This was, of course, only one aspect of the schism (made official by reciprocal excommunications in 1054), but it was perhaps the most overtly political one. For the Byzantines, Constantine's moving of the Empire's political capital from Rome to Constantinople in 332 meant that the ecclesiastical capital automatically *also* moved. However, the Byzantines regarded the Patriarch of Constantinople as *primus inter pares* ("first among equals") of the five patriarchates the Church was originally divided into: Alexandria, Antioch, Constantinople, Jerusalem, and Rome.
[19] *The City* — When Byzantines (and note again how often Eadric writes as though he were one) referred to *the* City, they always meant Constantinople.
[20] Bohemond III (r. 1164-1201). Bohemond put aside Theodora (the niece) shortly after Manuel's death in 1180, in order to pursue another woman.
[21] The importance these areas had had to the Empire in the past cannot be exaggerated — they had been the primary source of army recruits for centuries. The territorial losses of the later eleventh century (at least until Manuel's grandfather Alexius I (r.1081-1118) seized power and stopped the bleeding) were the real reason the Empire came to rely so much more heavily on foreign (mercenary) troops — the pool of "native" Byzantines had significantly dried up. Such conquest (or reconquest) would also extend Imperial control in southern Asia Minor to the Taurus Mountains, putting a formidable geographical barrier between the Empire and Saladin and/or any potentially hostile Crusaders.
[22] *Ballistae and mangonels* — variations of catapult.
[23] Here Eadric shows us that he meant what he said about his sister's knowledge of war. He expects her to understand that some of the requisite engines of siegecraft [*eg.* massive mobile wooden siege-towers covered with soaked hides to reduce their vulnerability to fire] would be built on site out of materials the Romans brought with them. The enemy, before retreating behind the city walls, would make certain that the surrounding countryside was devoid of anything the Romans could scavenge and press into service. The same would go for food (for the men) and fodder (for the animals). This was a *colossal* undertaking.
[24] Baldwin IV (r.1174-85), often called "the Leper King", as he suffered from that terrible disease.
[25] Baldwin of Antioch, brother to Maria of Antioch, the Empress.
[26] This is no exaggeration. Campaigning through western Turkey in the height of summer (in pre-modern times) was exactly as good an idea as invading Russia in the wintertime, although the extremes of weather and season-imposed hardship are, if I may be pardoned the expressions, polar opposites, literally hot and cold.
[27] Some of the most popular Byzantine "military saints". St. George, of course, was the renowned dragonslayer, while "Theodore" could have referred to either St. Theodore the Recruit or St. Theodore the Commander.
[28] Here I was tempted to insert a section break, and still very well might in the final edition.

It is clear that Eadric *did* take a break here; his handwriting improves for a couple of pages (indicating that he had rested, and was fresher), and there are some ink blotches on the manuscript, which I submit would be consistent with him having had some difficulty with the ink flow of his quill when he returned to work. And from here on out, he does digress a lot less, especially as his account becomes darker and more grim.

It should also be noted that the last sentence shows a strikingly modern viewpoint on Eadric's part — the idea that historical events do not take place in isolation, but are interconnected elements in a long chain of cause and effect.

[29] Dhū 'n Nūn.

[30] *I.e.*, Alexander the Great, when he invaded the Persian Empire.

[31] Eadric, well-informed as usual, is, in general, correct about the life-ways of these nomadic pastoralists. He likely wouldn't have been surprised to know that they, like the other groups he alludes to, originally came from the vast steppes of central Asia. Only, for a variety of reasons, these Turkic groups had turned south sooner, east of the Black Sea.

[32] *Marchwardens* — border guards. Here Eadric is merely using a term his sister would have been familiar with.

[33] Poisoning a well is a very simple operation. A dead animal (or even a person) is thrown down the well, usually with a few extra cuts or punctures added for good measure. Bacteria do the rest. Placing a carcass in a stream will also foul the water for some distance downstream from it. And when it came to streams, one rarely stooped at only one carcass.

[34] *Heathens* — Apparently Eadric does not believe the tribesmen to be Muslims, but rather some form of primitive idolaters, which is somewhat surprising for one as well-informed as he otherwise is.

[35] Of course, what Eadric is describing here is a severe outbreak of some form of dysenteric complaint, a bane which dogged the marches of all pre-modern armies. And, Manuel was essentially correct; this disease, suffered in the heat, and also with limited access to clean water, would, in the most extreme cases, kill its victims through severe dehydration. Most would recover, but be weakened considerably.

Animals of the types that accompanied the force were also susceptible to this type of affliction, although I cannot say at this juncture whether human and animal were infected from the same bacterial source, or whether this malady jumped species. Though not directly relevant to my subject here, given the sorry state of our world today with pandemics, etc., I intend to consult some colleagues in the medical sciences in order to provide more information (or at least better-educated guesses) in the definitive edition.

[36]For those interested, Haldon, *op. cit.* , *supra,* pp. 284-92, provides a detailed discussion of what is known regarding both the daily and overall provisioning of Byzantine armies.

[37] Here Eadric seems on the verge of a diatribe, but stops himself. He is alluding to the Byzantine military officer's professional assessment of the "Franks" or "Latins", as evidenced by several sources. While the westerners' prejudice against the "effeminate Greeks" is well-known and well-documented, the Byzantine view of them (saving that they were *barbaroi*) is less well-known.

Always careful not to waste resources, which is to say manpower, the Byzantines preferred to commit to battle only when the odds had been tilted as much as possible in their favour. (In other words, like all sanely-led modern armies!) A lot of that tilting was the result of their own espionage and diplomacy. The recommended method of dealing with a Latin force was to skirmish with it in such a way as to keep it in disadvantageous (amid physically uncomfortable) terrain, and to disrupt its supply lines. They viewed the Latins as undisciplined, and likely, just as Eadric implies, to desert or mutiny rather than stoically endure privation.

They were greatly respected as warriors, but not as soldiers who would remain at their posts no matter what. The heavy cavalry charge of the western chivalry was a terrifying thing, a juggernaut to avoid taking the brunt of if at all possible, but even it was a one-time "fire-and-forget" weapon. Once employed, the western horse units had neither the training, cohesion, nor discipline to reform for a second charge, or anything much other than break up into small uncoordinated melees. (To be fair, though , there more often than not wouldn't be any reason left to, as the Seljuks had first discovered to their cost at Dorylaeum in 1097. The Turks had made the fateful and never-to-be -repeated mistake of trying to face the knights of the First Crusade — weakened as they were by thirst and deprivation — directly on an open plain. The western horse carried all before it; the battle is reputed to have been over in twenty minutes.) But Byzantines and Saracens (whom the Byzantines respected above all other foes) could execute complex cavalry manoeuvres over the course of an engagement, again and again, the fruit of intense drilling.

So I suppose I have indulged in Eadric's diatribe for him. I do not apologize; as I stated at the outset, my very purpose in publishing this document is to provide a long-overdue corrective to the generally-held western view of Byzantium and her fighting-men.

[38] Manuel was fifty-six years old at the time of this campaign.

[39] Alexius I Comnenus (r.1081 – 1118)

[40] The military treatises with which Eadric was familiar with devoted chapter after chapter to counter-espionage stratagems for this and numerous other situations.

[41] *Jericho, Joshua.* Here Eadric is referring to the Biblical account of the walls of Jericho falling to the sound of the Israelites' trumpets in *Joshua, c.6.*

[42] *Tagma* – these were full-time, professional soldiers.

[43] Here of course, although the army has been compressed into a straight line due to the terrain, Eadric is referring to the section of the army which would be meant to take up its position to the right of the units forming the central body of the force when spread out on an open battlefield. In this case, that center was meant to be the *tagmatic* troops he has just mentioned above.

[44] A standard pre-modern infantry tactic was to place the greenest troops in the middle of a square, surrounded by more hardened troops, who would form the outer lines that would first clash with the enemy. Should the recruits panic, they would be surrounded by veterans who could steady them, or even forcibly restrain them from flight if necessary. Also, having more experienced troops in the rear line and sides of a square was critical in the event of a surprise suddenly appearing from any of those directions. Byzantine military treatises contain complex manoeuvres for both infantry and cavalry to shift their positions to meet new threats, and these drills were practiced regularly, at least by the full-time troops.

[45] *King Harold* – Harold Godwin, the Anglo-Saxon king of England defeated by William the Conqueror at the Battle of Hastings in 1066. Harold was killed by an arrow that struck him in the eye.

[46] *Men-at-arms* – These, too, would have been (heavier) infantry, as Baldwin would have kept his cavalry in the centre of his formation.

[47] *Greek Fire* – A Byzantine weapon the secret of whose exact composition was so closely guarded that it is still not precisely known. Often compared to napalm, it was hurled in tightly-sealed canisters that exposed their liquid contents to oxygen when they broke, causing them to ignite. Like gasoline, it would continue to burn even on the surface of water. Although it was used in sieges, it was primarily deployed as a naval weapon, as described above, or through a special siphon that acted as a kind of flamethrower. For obvious reasons, its constituent elements would be transported separately over long distances, to be prepared at or close to the site of intended use.

[48] Part of an attempt to train and equip a small, but elite cavalry unit that could match the Latins in sheer weight of armour.

[49] *Draughts* – Chess.

[50] A *decurion* was a leader of ten men. Here Eadric is telling us that it was the NCOs and older rankers who restored some measure of order.

[51] *Manumitted* – Freed.

[52] *Barding* – Horse armour.

[53] *High and blind* – While sheltering behind shields and horses, these bowmen would not have been able to pick targets and aim. They would simply have shot high into the air in the enemy's direction, and hoped the arrow came down on something, very much like early twentieth-century indirect artillery fire.

[54] The Archangel, often depicted in iconography as a warrior.

[55] *Padding beneath chainmail* – Chainmail's main purpose was to protect against slashing blades, and sometimes even deflected or snagged stabbing attacks. But it did nothing against blunt-force weapons like maces or clubs (or rocks); hence padding was worn underneath it.

[56] *Off-hand* – In this context, refers to the non-dominant hand.

[57] *"Varyagi na Tsarya!"* – Slavonic: "Varangians on the Emperor!"

[58] *Housecarl* – Household retainer, or man-at-arms.

[59] John II Comnenus (r.1118 – 43).

[60] *"Varyagi v pered!"* – "Varangians to the front!"

[61] *Beard* – Here Eadric is telling us that he was using a "bearded" axe. The "beard" refers to a one-and-a-half to two-inch extension of the bottom of the axe-blade, meant specifically as a hook for snagging weapons or limbs.

[62] Romanus V Diogenes (r. 1068 – 71), suffered a disastrous defeat at Manzikert (Aug. 17, 1071), due in large part to the treachery of *his* rearguard commander, Andronicus Ducas.

[63] *Circumcised and uncircumcised* – At this time, with only rare exceptions, the Turks would have been circumcised and the Christians not.

ABOUT THE AUTHOR

Stephen S. Bondar

Stephen S. Bondar has a Masters's Degree in Mediaeval Hiistory (Byzantine Empire), and is originally from Winnipeg, Canada.

Made in United States
Orlando, FL
03 January 2024

42101343R00067